Mostly Ghostly

Freaks and Shrieks

7

Experience all the chills of the Mostly Ghostly series!

AND COMING SOON:

Mostly Ghostly 7

Freaks and Shrieks

R.L. STINE

DELACORTE PRESS
A PARACHUTE PRESS BOOK

Published by
Delacorte Press
an imprint of
Random House Children's Books
a division of Random House, Inc.
New York

Visit us on the Web! www.randomhouse.com/kids
Educators and librarians, for a variety of teaching tools,
visit us at www.randomhouse.com/teachers

Library of Congress Cataloging-in-Publication Data
Stine, R.L.
Freaks and shrieks / R.L. Stine
p. cm. — (Mostly ghostly)
Summary: When Max makes a deal with the two ghosts inhabiting his
bedroom in order to find out how these friends became spirits, he must
switch brains with the only witness to the event, a chimpanzee.
ISBN 0-385-74694-6 (trade) — ISBN 0-385-90932-2 (glb)
[1. Ghosts—Fiction. 2. Brain—Fiction. 3. Chimpanzees—Fiction.
4. Magic—Fiction.] I. Title.
PZ7.S86037Fre 2005
[Fic]—dc22
2005008633

Printed in the United States of America

August 2005

10 9 8 7 6 5 4 3 2 1

BVG

i

MY SISTER, TARA, AND I were arguing. For a change.

"You didn't have to throw the fish up in the air," I said. "You got Max into a lot of trouble."

"It was a joke, Nicky," Tara said. "It was supposed to be funny."

"Max didn't think it was funny," I said. "And what about the rest of the class? When the fish cracked in half, those poor kids started screaming their heads off."

"That's what made it funny," Tara replied. She jammed her floppy red hat down over her dark hair.

It was a sunny, warm afternoon. Tara and I were walking home from Max's school.

Tara and I don't have a school of our own to go to. That's because we're dead.

We're ghosts.

Max Doyle is the only person we know who can see and hear us. Sometimes being a ghost is lonely and boring. So Tara and I follow Max to school and try to help him out.

Today we didn't help him out much.

Today was Pet Day in Ms. McDonald's sixth-grade class. But Max didn't want to bring his big, furry wolfhound, Buster, to school. That's because Buster *hates* Max.

Buster starts to growl and snap whenever Max comes near. When he sees Max, he only thinks, Meat! Max gets a little tired of having his dog chew on him all the time.

So Max didn't bring Buster for Pet Day. Instead, he did a very funny thing. He brought a big fish to school. A dead one. It was the stuffed bass that his dad had mounted on the den wall.

Max pulled the fish off the wall and carried it to class. When it was his turn, he carried it to the front of the room. He told everyone it was his pet fish, Ernie.

That's when Tara decided to help Max out.

I tried to stop her. But my sister is stubborn. Once Tara makes up her mind to do something, forget it. That's why I call her Hurricane Tara.

She floated up to the front of the room and took the fish from Max's hands. "Maxie, let me hold it up while you describe it," she said.

"No—give it back!" Max cried. He made a grab for the fish—and missed.

A lot of kids in the class were kinda shocked.

They couldn't see Tara. They could only see the fish jumping out of Max's hands. Max seemed to be standing there arguing with *himself*!

"Give it back!" Max shouted again. He grabbed the tail and tugged.

Tara tugged back. "I'm only trying to make your talk more interesting," she said.

It became a real tug-of-war.

Ms. MacDonald's mouth dropped open. "Max—what are you doing?"

"Trying to reel him in," Max said. "He's . . . uh . . . trying to swim upstream."

Some kids were laughing hard now.

Tara should have stopped. But my little sister doesn't know the words "give up."

"Nicky! Catch!" she shouted. And she tossed the big fish high in the air. Over the kids' heads to me at the back of the room.

"It's okay, everyone!" Max shouted. "It's a *flying* fish!"

Tara threw it too hard. It bounced off the chalkboard, sailed back, and hit a girl in the head.

She started to scream.

The bass hit the floor hard—and broke in half. Hundreds of cockroaches poured out from inside it, scampering over the floor.

And then *everyone* was screaming. Screaming, stamping their feet, leaping onto their chairs.

It was way funny. But no one was laughing.

Max was in major trouble. Tara and I decided it was time to leave.

So now we were walking past sparkling green front yards, on our way back to Max's house. Our old house—when we were alive.

"Max didn't look too happy," I said.

Tara sighed. "I was only trying to make Pet Day more fun. It's hard to have fun when you're . . . when you're a ghost."

Two squirrels came chasing each other across the grass. They ran right between Tara and me. One of them brushed my leg. They had no idea we were there.

"Yeah. I hate being invisible," I said. "I'm tired of being a ghost. I wish Mom and Dad would hurry back."

Our parents are ghosts too. We don't know why. We don't know what happened to our family.

Mom and Dad were scientists. They had a lab where they found a way to capture evil ghosts. One day, the ghosts escaped. And the four of us were no longer alive.

That's all we know.

Mom and Dad went off to find answers. They think they can find a way to bring our family back to life. They told us to wait for them in our old house, with Max and his family.

But they've been gone a *long* time. Tara and I really miss them. We've been feeling very sad lately.

We turned onto Bleek Street, our street. I heard shouts from the next yard. A boy was screaming.

Tara and I hurried across the street. We saw the Wilbur brothers, Billy and Willy—the worst kids at Jefferson Elementary.

They were teasing a little red-haired boy. He looked to be only five or six.

Billy Wilbur grabbed the boy's baseball cap and tossed it to his brother, Willy. They were playing keep-away with the little guy's cap. They held it right in front of his face, then jerked it out of his reach.

The little boy started to cry. That made the Wilbur brothers toss back their heads and hee-haw with laughter.

"Come on, Nicky." Tara tugged my arm. "Let's go have a little fun with those Wilbur brats."

2

BILLY WILBUR HAD THE little boy's cap. He squatted down at the edge of a flower garden and started scooping with one hand, filling the cap with mud.

"Give me my cap!" the little boy pleaded. Tears ran down his red cheeks. "It's my new cap!"

"It's *our* new cap now!" Willy said.

Billy stood up and whirled around. He raised the cap, brimming with mud. "You want it back, Casey?" he said, grinning. "Okay, I'll give it back."

"Put it back on Casey's head," Willy said, grinning at his brother.

Tara swooped up behind them. She grabbed the cap and plopped it down on Billy Wilbur's head. The wet mud oozed down his face.

Casey's mouth dropped open in surprise.

Billy turned angrily to his brother. "Hey, punk! Whatja do that for?" He pulled the cap off and tossed it at Willy. He wiped mud off his face with one hand and smeared it down the front of his brother's shirt.

"Hey!" Willy jumped back. "I didn't do anything!"

I grabbed him by the shoulders and made him spin around a few times. Tara had ahold of Billy. We pushed them forward and made them crack heads.

They both cried out angrily.

Casey laughed.

"What's your problem?" Billy Wilbur shouted angrily.

"What's *your* problem?" Willy screamed.

They both turned on little Casey. "What are you laughing about, punk?" Willy snarled. "It's time for your mud bath, isn't it?"

Casey stumbled back.

"Yeah," Billy agreed. "Mud bath time."

"Nooooo—please!" Casey screamed.

They both dove at him. But Tara and I grabbed the two Wilburs by their ankles.

"Whoa—!"

"Hey!"

We pulled them up till they were standing on their heads.

Casey stared at them in shock. "How do you do that?" he asked.

"I . . . don't . . . know," Billy Wilbur said.

"I can't get down!" his brother groaned. "Casey, help us down!"

Casey stood there frozen, gaping at them.

Then he grabbed his muddy cap and took off running down the block.

As soon as he was gone, Tara and I let go of the Wilburs. They flopped onto their stomachs, confused. Then they both jumped up fast.

They gazed all around. They scratched their heads.

"Weird," Willy Wilbur muttered.

"Totally," his brother said.

They took off running in the other direction.

Tara and I laughed. "That was kinda fun," I said.

"Too easy," Tara replied. "Hey, Nicky. Maybe that's what we could be doing for laughs. Turn everyone upside down! *Terrorize* the neighborhood!"

I nodded. "Well . . . we're already terrorizing Max!"

"He'll like what we did to the Wilburs," Tara said, straightening her cap. "If he ever speaks to us again."

We crossed the street. Our house was two blocks away. A girl raced past on a bike, pedaling furiously. She almost knocked us over. She had no idea we were there.

I heard footsteps on the sidewalk behind us.

I spun around—and saw a short man. Cropped white beard. Wearing a black raincoat.

He slid behind a fat tree trunk.

"Weird," I muttered.

Tara and I walked another half block. Again, I heard the scrape of shoes on the walk behind us.

We both turned around. I saw a flash of black—the man's raincoat disappearing as he ducked behind a hedge.

I stared hard at the hedge. I could see the man ducking low, peering back at us.

A chill ran down my back.

I turned to my sister. "Tara," I whispered, "guess what? We're being followed."

3

TARA TURNED AND SQUINTED into the hedge. "Let's go see what he wants," she said.

She tugged her hat down and started walking toward the man, swinging her arms at her sides.

Typical.

I ran after her and grabbed her by the shoulders. "Hel-*lo*! Are you *crazy*? Don't you see him hiding there?"

She pulled herself free. "So?"

"So he doesn't want us to see him," I said, glancing back at him. I could see the black raincoat through the leafy hedge. "That means he's dangerous," I said. "How many dangerous ghosts have come after us this year?"

"A lot," Tara replied. "What makes you think he's a ghost?"

I let out a sigh. "I don't know *what* he is. I only know he's trying hard not to be seen."

"Then, if you're so smart, what should we do?" Tara asked.

I thought about it for a moment. "Run?"

"Okay. Run," Tara said.

We took off running side by side across the grass.

Two squirrels turned their heads as we zoomed past. I knew they couldn't see us, but they must have felt the burst of wind.

Some kid had left a tricycle in his driveway, and I ran right through it. Tara's long plastic earrings jangled and flew behind her as she picked up speed.

We reached the end of the block. I glanced back.

The man was still following. His black raincoat flapped in the wind. He dove around the side of a house when he saw me turn.

"Almost home," I said. "We'll be safe." I started across the street—but Tara tugged me to a stop.

"No. Not home," she said, breathing hard. "We can't go home, Nicky. We don't want him to know where we live."

The man peeked out at us from behind the house, then quickly pulled his head back.

"Okay. Let's go." I turned at the corner and led us away from our house. We ran into a backyard with a small plastic swimming pool and pool toys scattered everywhere.

We ran to the side of the garage and stopped. "Is he still there?" Tara asked.

I peeked out. "Yes. Still there."

"Let's go into this house," Tara said. She had her hands on her knees and was struggling to catch her breath. "Maybe it will throw him off the track. He'll think it's our house."

"Maybe," I said. "Or maybe he'll come in after us."

Tara didn't wait to discuss it. She disappeared through the brick wall of the house, and I followed her inside.

We found ourselves in a brightly lit yellow and white kitchen. Two little boys sat at a small kitchen table. One of them was playing with a Game Boy. The other was coloring with markers.

They didn't look up when Tara and I burst inside.

Tara stepped right up to their table. "Hey, guys, can you hear us?" she called.

No.

Tara and I tiptoed to the kitchen window. My heart was pounding. We *never* sneak into other people's houses. It just doesn't seem right.

But this was definitely an emergency.

We both leaned on the edge of the kitchen sink and peered out the window. "Oh, wow!" Tara cried. "Look at him. He's still out there!"

The little man looked angry. Above his short white beard, his face was bright red. He stood beside the kiddie pool, his eyes narrowed into slits.

He had his hands shoved into the pockets of the raincoat.

He stared at the house. But he didn't make a move to come inside.

"Who is he?" Tara whispered. "Why is he following us?"

I sighed. "It can't be *good* news."

"Level Three!" the kid with the Game Boy shouted from behind us at the table. "I made it to Level Three!"

I watched the little man start to pace back and forth. I could see he was thinking hard. He nearly fell into the swimming pool!

He took a few steps toward the back door.

My heart skipped a beat. Tara grabbed my arm. "Nicky—is he coming in?"

No.

He seemed to change his mind. He spun around and walked off. I stretched up as far as I could, watching him stride away.

I let out a long breath of air and stepped back from the window. "I . . . I think he's gone," I said. "But let's wait a few minutes to make sure."

I saw a plate of Girl Scout cookies on the counter. Thin Mints. My favorite.

"Don't even think about it," Tara said. She shivered. "We have to get home. I *hate* being followed. I didn't like that little man."

I couldn't resist. I lifted one cookie off the plate.

Wouldn't you know it? That's when both little boys turned around.

They saw the cookie floating in midair. And they both started to laugh. They thought it was funny.

I popped the cookie into my mouth.

"Mommy—the cookies are *alive*!" one of the kids shouted. "The cookies *fly*!"

"Way to go, dude," Tara said. "Come on. We're outta here." She pulled me through the kitchen wall.

Outside, we pressed ourselves against the brick wall. Staying in the shadow of the house, we gazed around.

No sign of the little man.

"Let's move," Tara whispered.

We took off, running hard. I was gasping for breath by the time we reached our house. Tara and I burst right through the front door without bothering to open it.

We didn't stop to see if anyone was home. We bolted up the front stairs—to Max's room.

"Max? Are you home?" I shouted. "Max?"

And there stood someone in black. Waiting for us.

4

PANTING HARD, I STAGGERED back against the wall. Was it the little man? No. Not the guy with the white beard. It was Max's big brother, Colin.

Colin, dressed in black sweats, snooping around Max's room.

He pulled open Max's desk drawers and pawed through the stuff inside. What was he looking for?

Probably just snooping.

Colin is not the best big brother in the world. Actually, he might be the *worst*.

Colin is big and handsome and blond and strong and athletic. He works out all the time. And he uses chubby little Max as a crash test dummy.

"Ooh. What's that smell?" Tara whispered. She pinched her fingers over her nose.

"Why are you whispering?" I asked. "Colin can't hear us." And then I smelled it too. Something sour.

A *really* sour smell. Like two-day-old puke.

Colin carried a little white paper bag over to Max's bed. He checked the door to make sure no one was coming. Then he reached inside the bag and pulled out an egg.

Whoa. The disgusting odor swept over us. It was coming from the egg!

Colin had a cold grin on his face. He held the egg way out in front of him.

Holding my nose, I moved closer. The egg was hard-boiled and covered in mold. Furry green and blue stuff had grown all over it.

Totally gross.

And what did Colin plan to do with the rotten egg?

Put it under Max's pillow, of course.

"Let's stop him," Tara whispered. She was fading in and out of view. I could barely see her.

"I can't," I said. "I'm feeling . . . very . . . weak."

That's one problem with being a ghost. If you use your energy up, you disappear for a while. Sometimes a short while. Sometimes a long while.

You can't control it.

It's like you're asleep. Only you don't know where you are. And you never dream.

I felt myself dissolving, fading away. . . .

I saw Colin slide the rotten egg under Max's pillow. I watched him hurry out of the room.

"Later, Tara," I whispered. "I'm . . . fading . . . fast."

"Me . . . too," she whispered. And then before we disappeared, she quickly added, "Know what's so totally scary about that guy who chased us? *He could* see *us!*"

5

"Yo, Aaron. It's Max. What's up?"

I pressed the cell phone to my ear and gazed around my room. Something smelled bad. I wondered if Nicky and Tara were up to more evil tricks.

They totally messed me up in school today. And they broke my dad's precious wall bass in half. How would I ever explain it to him?

I never told Dad I was taking it. My plan had been to borrow it, then get it back up on the den wall before he came home from work.

Well, forget about that. I was in deep doo-doo.

And now my two ghost friends were hiding somewhere. Afraid to face me—and I didn't blame them.

But what was that yucko smell?

"Aaron, where were you?" I asked. "It's almost dinnertime. You were supposed to come here this afternoon, remember? We were going to print out this month's newsletter for our *Stargate SG-1* club."

18

On the other end of the line, I heard Aaron shout something to his mother. Then he came back on. "I got grounded, Max," he said.

"Oh, wow," I muttered. "Not again."

Aaron is my best buddy in the whole world. But I don't see him too often. That's because he spends almost his entire life grounded.

"This time it's pretty bad," he said. "And it's all because of a science experiment."

"Excuse me?" I said. "Dude, what kind of science experiment?"

"I was testing the strength of different glues. You know. Every glue has a different stickiness to it. I wanted to see what kind of glue was the stickiest."

I waited to hear the rest. "Go on, Aaron," I said finally.

"Well . . . to make a long story short, I glued my sister's sneakers to the floor."

"Kaytlin's sneakers?" I cried. "Was she *in* them when you glued them?"

"No. She wasn't home," Aaron said. "Hey, I'm not stupid, dude. I wouldn't glue her sneakers to the floor if she was *in* them!"

"And how did you pull them up off the floor?" I asked.

"Couldn't," Aaron replied. "That's why I'm *so* doomed. I used the strongest glue. Those sneakers will never come up."

"Oh, wow," I muttered again.

"And one more bad thing," Aaron said.

"What's that?" I asked.

"They're glued down right in the middle of the living room."

I let out another groan. I felt sorry for Aaron. He was a really good guy. He just could never resist doing science experiments on stuff that belonged to his little sister.

And he always got caught.

"So you're grounded for life again?" I asked.

"My parents are really angry. They say I'm not fit to live in the house," Aaron said. "I have to live in a tent in the backyard. I'm only allowed inside for meals."

"That's harsh," I said. "What if you have to go to the bathroom?"

"Uh-oh," he said. "I didn't think about that."

"I guess the *Stargate* newsletter will have to wait," I said.

"Well, Max, since you and I are the only members of the club, it can probably wait."

"I have major news to tell you," I said.

"Major news?"

"I mean, this may be the *biggest*, most totally exciting news of my life!" I said.

"More exciting than when you met that girl who knows Hilary Duff's cousin?"

"Aaron, this news is so totally unbelievable—"

I stopped because I heard a scream.

Aaron's scream on the other end of the phone.

A shrill, earsplitting screech of horror.

"Aaron? What's wrong?" I cried. "What happened? What's *wrong*?"

6

"MY AIR! MY AIR!" he wailed.

I gasped. I nearly dropped the phone. "Aaron? What's wrong? No air? You can't *breathe*?"

"No!" he cried. "I said my *ear*! My *ear*! It's totally stuck!"

"Huh? I don't understand," I replied. "What about your ear?"

"Kaytlin did it!" Aaron shouted. "Ouch. She did it. She got her revenge. My *ear*! She put glue on my cell phone. It's . . . it's stuck to my ear!"

"Take it easy," I said. "Take a deep breath. Then, very gently, try to slide it off."

"It's stuck on," Aaron said. "She really did it to me this time. It's stuck on for life!"

"Let me tell you my big news—" I started, trying to take his mind off his cell phone problem.

"*Your* big news?" he cried. "How about *my* big news? I'm going to have a phone hanging from my ear for the rest of my life!"

I heard Mom calling me down to dinner. "I've

got to go," I said. Aaron was screaming so loudly, I don't think he heard me. "Call you later," I said.

"Great. I'll be here—right by the phone!" he screamed.

I clicked my cell phone off, slipped it into my jeans pocket, and hurried down to the kitchen.

Mom, Dad, and Colin were already sitting at the table. "I didn't have time to cook," Mom said. "So we're having submarine sandwiches."

"Awesome," I said.

As I started to take my seat next to Colin, he picked up my plate and slid it onto my chair.

I couldn't stop myself. I sat on my sandwich.

Colin hee-hawed. "Gotcha again, little bro!"

Dad laughed too. He thinks Colin is a riot. "Hey, Max," he boomed, "which end do you eat with?"

He and Colin yukked it up, laughing and pounding the table with their fists.

"That's not funny," Mom said. Even though Colin and Dad gang up on me, Mom usually takes my side. "You shouldn't ruin good food, even for a joke."

"It isn't ruined," I said. I put my plate on the table. "It's just a little flat."

Colin reached into my sandwich and pulled out some lettuce. He stuffed the lettuce up my nose.

"That's not funny at all," Mom said.

"Yes it is," Colin replied. "It looks like snot."

He and Dad hee-hawed some more.

I didn't care. I was too excited about my big news.

"I have the most *amazing* news," I said.

"Max, don't talk with a lettuce leaf in your nose," Mom said.

"Oh. Sorry." I pulled out the lettuce. "Listen to my news. Ballantine is coming to town!"

All three of them stared at me. "Who?" Mom and Dad asked at the same time.

"Ballantine," I repeated. "You know. Ballantine the Nearly Amazing?"

"He's a magician?" Mom asked.

"Only one of the most famous magicians in the world!" I exclaimed. "He's coming to our town. And he's holding open auditions for young magicians."

Colin giggled. "Maybe he'll wave his wand and make you disappear."

"It's an *awesome* opportunity," I said, ignoring my brother. "Ballantine is taking on three students. He's going to teach them and help them with their magic. And if he chooses me . . ."

I stopped talking. I saw something float toward the dinner table.

An egg.

Nicky or Tara must be carrying it, I realized.

It smelled sour and pukey.

It must have been the egg that smelled so bad in my room, I realized. A rotten egg.

I watched as it floated toward Colin.

"That is very exciting," Mom said. "You'd better practice hard, Max."

The rotten egg lowered itself toward Colin's plate.

"If Ballantine likes me, I could be the next big magic star!" I said. "I could be on TV and everything."

"We all could come watch you perform," Mom said.

I watched the egg slide into Colin's submarine sandwich.

Colin didn't see it. He slapped me on the back, so hard that my eyeballs practically flew out of my head.

"Hey, Maxie, what stinks in here?" He sniffed me. "You need to take a shower," he said.

He lifted the sub with both hands. "I can do magic, too. Watch this sandwich disappear before your eyes!" Then he shoved it into his mouth and began chomping away.

The sandwich was almost gone when he suddenly stopped his loud, furious chewing and swallowing.

A sick look of horror spread over his face. He turned green. Really! Pale green.

"I'm . . . going . . . to . . . hurl!" he murmured.

Holding both hands over his mouth, he jumped up and tore out of the room.

I wanted to laugh. But I turned and saw Dad glaring at me angrily. "Max," he boomed, "see what you did? Why did you make your brother eat so fast? You made him sick!"

7

"MAX, WHERE ARE YOU going?"

I had just stepped out the front door and started down the driveway when I heard Tara call me.

It was a damp, warmish Saturday morning. Gray clouds rolled low overhead. Gusts of wind sent the flowers in our little garden bending one way, then the other.

"Hey, Max—wait up!" Nicky called.

"Not now. I'm in a hurry," I said. I still hadn't forgiven them for the bass incident on Pet Day.

Nicky and Tara appeared at my sides. Tara grabbed my arm. "Maxie, we haven't had any time to hang out. Are we still friends?"

"I don't have time to hang out right now," I said. "I have to get to the magic store in town. I'm going to audition for Ballantine the Nearly Amazing. I'm going to show him my best card tricks."

I felt the deck of trick cards in my jeans pocket. I was so nervous, I'd almost forgotten them.

"Wow." Nicky shook his head. "Dude, that's big. That's way big."

"Bye," I said. I moved away from them and started to hurry down the street. Mom couldn't drive me, so I had to take the Miller Street bus into town.

"Don't be tense," Tara said, floating after me. They both hovered two or three inches above the ground. "What happens if you pass the test today?"

"Today is like a pretest," I said. "Today I only get to do one trick. If he likes it, I get to do a *real* performance for him later."

"You are *so* there," Nicky said. "He'll like you."

"Yes, you're going to totally impress him," Tara said, taking my arm again. "Know why?"

I squinted at her. "Why?"

"Because we're gonna help you!" Tara replied.

"Oh no!" I screamed, spinning around to face them. *"No way!"*

"Maxie, calm down," Tara said.

I started to jog. "You're gonna make me miss the bus."

"You know we can help you," Nicky insisted, floating after me. He was at least a foot off the ground now.

I suddenly wished I could fly too. I'd fly away from *them*!

"Max, we'll make things float for you," Tara said. "We'll make things fly up in the air."

"Yeah," Nicky agreed. "When we finish doing our tricks, Ballantine's head will be *spinning!*"

"Ooh—that's a good trick!" Tara exclaimed. "Maybe we could make Ballantine's head spin around a few times. *That* would impress him!"

"I don't want his head to spin," I said through gritted teeth. I stopped jogging and turned to face them.

"I have to do this on my own," I said. "You understand that, don't you? You're my friends. I know you only want to help. But you always manage to mess things up, and—"

I realized they weren't listening to me. They were staring over my shoulder. They both suddenly looked very frightened.

"What's wrong?" I asked.

"There he is again," Nicky whispered.

"Who?" I asked. I spun around. I didn't see anyone.

"He's following us," Tara said. "You can't see him. He ducked behind that mailbox."

I blinked. "Someone is following you? Someone else can *see* you?"

They both nodded.

"On the count of three," Tara said, "we run. Ready?"

I stared at the mailbox. I saw someone peek

out from behind it. A man with a white beard. Dressed in black.

"Onetwothree," Tara whispered in one breath.

We took off. All three of us, running full speed down the sidewalk.

We jumped over a kid's bike lying across the walk, kept running, and crossed onto Miller. Squinting into the gray light, I could see the bus several blocks down.

I started to point to it. Then stopped when I saw the man in the black raincoat leap up behind us.

"*No!*" I screamed.

But he grabbed Nicky and Tara, one in each hand.

"Gotcha," he growled.

8

"LET GO OF THEM!" I shouted.

I wanted to rush the guy. Maybe tackle him so he'd let my friends loose.

He wasn't very big. But something about him frightened me.

And there was one thing holding me back. I'm a total coward.

So instead of rushing him, I took a few steps away. I realized I was trembling all over.

He stared at me with bright blue eyes, round as marbles, under bushy white eyebrows. His white hair and short white beard were neatly trimmed. His face was wrinkled and red from running after us.

"Let us go!"

Nicky and Tara were both struggling and squirming to free themselves.

The man was breathing hard. But he kept his tight grip on them.

"Let us go!"

"I'm here to help you," he said. He had a thin

whisper of a voice. "Stop fighting me. I'm your friend."

"Then let us go!" Nicky shouted again.

"Okay. No problem." The man opened his hands and released my two friends.

Nicky and Tara jumped away from him.

I stood studying the little man. Was he telling the truth? Was he a friend?

"How come you can see us?" Nicky demanded.

"If you are our friend, why have you been following us?" Tara asked.

"I wanted to make sure I had the right kids," the man replied. "I didn't want to scare you. But I had to be absolutely sure."

"Why do you want us? Why should we believe you?" Nicky asked.

I watched the Miller Street bus rumble past. I let out a sigh. Okay. I'll catch the next one, I decided. They come by every half hour.

"I can't answer your questions out here," the man told Nicky and Tara. "You must trust me. And you must come with me—now."

9

"**TRUST YOU? WHY SHOULD** we trust you?" Tara cried. "Let's go, Nicky. Max." She tugged her brother away.

The little man turned his shiny blue eyes on her. "I worked with your parents," he said softly.

Nicky and Tara stopped and turned around.

"My name is Dr. Samuel Smollet," the man said. "I'm a scientist. And an expert in the spirit world. I worked with your parents on their ghost project."

Nicky and Tara studied him. I started to feel a little calmer. The man seemed kindly and sincere. I took a deep breath and let it out slowly.

"You knew our parents?" Tara asked.

He nodded. "I was there when they started their ghost experiments. I helped them capture evil ghosts and hold them prisoner."

The wind made his raincoat flap behind him. He wore a black suit underneath it, a white shirt with a stiff collar, and a plain blue tie.

"Your parents are brilliant scientists," he

said. "Oh. Sorry. I mean they *were* brilliant scientists."

"And what do you want with Nicky and Tara?" I asked.

He kept his eyes on them. "I think I can help you," he said.

"Help us? How?" Tara hung back. I could tell she was still suspicious.

Dr. Smollet rubbed his beard. "Where are your parents?" he asked. "I can help them, too."

Nicky kicked a clump of dirt off the sidewalk. "We don't know where they went," he said. "They've been gone a long time."

Tara crossed her arms in front of her chest. "How can you help us?" she demanded.

A smile slowly spread over Dr. Smollet's face, making his cheeks wrinkle. "I have someone with me. At my lab," he said. "His name is Mr. Harvey. I believe he can help bring you back to life."

Nicky and Tara both gasped.

"You're kidding," Tara blurted out.

Dr. Smollet's smile faded. "I'm not kidding. I think I know how to do it. I wish your parents were here. I owe them a lot. I want to help them."

Nicky sighed. "I wish they were here too," he murmured.

I felt the deck of cards in my pocket. Ballantine the Nearly Amazing was already at the magic store. I wanted to get there to perform for him.

Tara still had her arms crossed. "How can you bring us back to life?" she asked Dr. Smollet.

He pulled his raincoat around him. "I can't do it here in the middle of the street," he said, glancing around. "I need for you to come to my lab."

"Where's your lab?" Nicky asked.

Dr. Smollet pointed with his head. "On the other side of town," he said. "I'll take you there. You can meet Mr. Harvey. Then you can decide if you want me to help you."

Tara pulled back. "You're a total stranger. You want us to go with you?"

Dr. Smollet shrugged. "I only want to help you. If your parents were here, they would tell you to trust me. I don't know what else I can say."

He pointed again. "My lab is just on the other side of town. You only have to stay a few minutes to meet Mr. Harvey. Then I will take you anywhere you want to go."

Nicky, Tara, and I huddled on the curb. I heard a cat crying from the house behind us. An SUV rolled past, loud rap music blasting from its open windows.

"Is this guy for real?" Tara whispered.

"I think he's telling the truth," Nicky said.

I glanced at Dr. Smollet. "It might be some kind of trap," I said.

"If it is a trap, Nicky and I will just go invisible," Tara said. "No problem."

"It's one of the good things about being a ghost," Nicky said.

"If he *is* telling the truth," I said, "this could be an awesome day for you. This is what you've been praying for!"

"I don't want to get excited yet," Nicky said. "But I am. I really am. If this scientist really knows how to return us to life . . ."

He started jumping up and down. He couldn't hold back his excitement.

Tara grabbed Nicky by the shoulders and held him down. "Don't get your hopes up."

"Too late," Nicky said. "My hopes are already up. I can't *wait* to be alive again!"

Tara turned to me. "Nicky and I will go with Dr. Smollet," she said. "But you don't have to take the risk, Max. Go to the magic store. You don't want to be late for your audition."

"But—" I started.

Tara stepped up to Dr. Smollet. "Nicky and I will go with you to your lab," she said. "But Max has other things to do in town."

Dr. Smollet frowned and shook his head. He raised his blue eyes to me. "Oh no," he said softly. "That won't do."

He motioned for me to follow him. "You come too, Max. We need you. You're going to be *very* important."

10

DR. SMOLLET'S LAB WAS in a three-story white stucco building. A barbed wire fence surrounded the place. I saw empty lots on both sides. No stores or houses on the block.

He opened the gate with a key and led us to the white front door. I saw rows of tiny windows rising up to the flat red roof. All the windows were barred.

As soon as we stepped inside, I heard the shrill cries.

Animal cries. Shrieks and howls. Muffled behind a long row of closed doors.

Dr. Smollet noticed my surprise. "Don't pay any attention," he said. "We do a lot of animal experiments here. The animals are all well cared for."

We started down a long white hall. Even the carpet was white. The animal cries became fainter as we turned a corner that led into another white hall.

Nicky and Tara glanced around nervously. "Did our parents work here?" Tara asked.

37

Dr. Smollet nodded. He led us into a big square room filled with computer equipment. The walls were solid white. Bright lights beamed down from the low ceiling.

I saw rows of laptops on two long tables. Cables stretched above our heads. Large electronic machines beeped and hummed against one wall. Red and blue lights blinked.

Flat-screen monitors filled another wall. The monitors flashed numbers and equations and formulas.

Dr. Smollet pulled off his raincoat and suit jacket and tossed them on a chair. He tugged down the sleeves of his starched white shirt.

I could still hear the animal shrieks in the distance. Sad, frightened cries. They made me feel frightened too.

Had we made a big mistake?

I swallowed hard. My mouth was suddenly very dry, and my hands felt as cold as ice. I jammed them into my jeans pockets—and felt the deck of trick cards.

Will I get out of here in time to see Ballantine?

The lab was neat and clean. The monitors blinked silently. The big electronic machines clicked and hummed. Dr. Smollet smiled as the three of us gazed around.

"This lab belonged to your parents," he told

Nicky and Tara. "This is where they worked. And I worked here alongside them."

"Wow," Nicky said, shaking his head. He walked up to a long table of laptops. "I think I remember being here. It's a faint memory. But it's coming back to me."

"Yes, I remember the computers," Tara said. "And all those wires and cables on the ceiling."

She tugged at her dangling plastic earrings. She always pulled them when she was thinking hard or trying to remember something.

"We were here, Nicky," she said. "I know we were. Why can't I remember it better?"

Dr. Smollet leaned on the table with his hands. "That's what we're here to find out," he said.

He pointed to the machines against the wall. "Your parents and I worked here, capturing evil ghosts. Your parents were on a mission. They believed that a lot of the evil in the world was caused by these spirits. Your parents found a way to capture them and keep them prisoner here."

Dr. Smollet sighed. "But one evil ghost—a man named Phears—escaped. I tried to fight him off. But he was too powerful for me. He injured me. He knocked me out. When I came to, *all* the evil ghosts had escaped. Phears had freed them all."

"We—we've run into Phears," Nicky said.

Dr. Smollet's blue eyes grew wide. "You and

your sister were here in the lab on that awful day. Don't you remember? Don't you understand?"

Nicky and Tara froze. They stared at him. Speechless.

"We . . . didn't know," Tara said finally.

"You were visiting your parents here," Dr. Smollet said. "When Phears escaped, he did something to your family. To all four of you."

"You were here," I said. "Didn't you see what happened to them?"

Dr. Smollet shook his head. "No. I didn't see anything. I was out cold."

He took a deep breath and smoothed back his white hair. "But I have someone here who saw everything," he said. "I have a witness. I told you his name. Mr. Harvey."

"Where is he?" Tara asked.

Nicky strode up to Dr. Smollet. "Can we talk to him? Is he here now?"

Dr. Smollet nodded. "Mr. Harvey is the only one who saw everything that happened that day. He saw Phears escape. He saw Phears free the other ghosts. And he saw what Phears did to you and your parents."

The scientist loosened his tie. It was cool in the lab, but beads of sweat rolled down his forehead.

"Mr. Harvey *may* know the secret. He may know how to bring your family back to life," he said, gazing intently at my two ghost friends.

"Please—can we see him?" Tara cried. "Can we talk to him now?"

Dr. Smollet cleared his throat. He tugged at his tie again. "Well . . . there's a small problem. I'll show you."

He swung away from the table and walked quickly out of the lab. The door closed behind him.

Nicky and Tara stared at each other. Then they turned to me.

"I . . . I don't know what to say," Tara confessed. "I'm shaking!"

"Me too," Nicky said, his voice cracking. He pumped his fists in the air. "This is too good to be true. Do you think Mr. Harvey really can bring us back to life? And tell us what happened to us?"

The lab door swung open.

Dr. Smollet stepped in, followed by another figure.

"This is Mr. Harvey," Dr. Smollet said.

Tara's mouth dropped open.

Nicky gasped.

I stared hard at Mr. Harvey. My brain felt as if it was spinning in my head. "But . . . but . . . ," I stammered. "Mr. Harvey is a *chimp*!"

11

DR. SMOLLET LED THE chimp by the hand.

Mr. Harvey loped into the room, bouncing as he walked. He kept shaking his head, his lips moving silently. Then he pulled back his lips and gave us a toothy grin.

The chimp was about three feet tall. He wore bright red spandex bike shorts. He had a red baseball cap on his head. But as he crossed the room toward us, he pulled the cap off and tossed it across the lab.

"Hoo hoo hoo." He made chimp noises and bobbed up and down, his hands on his hairy knees.

Tara stormed up to Dr. Smollet angrily. "Is this some kind of stupid joke?" she demanded.

Nicky pulled Tara back. "Let's go," he muttered. "This is totally insane."

"No, wait—" the scientist said. He petted the back of the chimp's head. Mr. Harvey flashed us another grin.

"I told you there was a problem," Dr. Smollet said.

"How could you do that to them?" I cried. "How could you get their hopes up like that?" I felt as disappointed as Nicky and Tara.

"Please let me explain," Dr. Smollet said. He lifted Mr. Harvey onto a tall wooden lab stool at the counter. The chimp reached out and started to play with Dr. Smollet's white hair.

Dr. Smollet pulled the chimp's hand away. "Be a good boy, Mr. Harvey. This is a big day for you," he said.

He turned to us. "Yes, Mr. Harvey is a chimp. But he was here in the lab when Phears escaped. He saw what happened to you and your parents. He was the only witness."

"But he *can't talk*!" Tara screamed.

"Hoo hoo hoo," Mr. Harvey said. He reached for Dr. Smollet's hair again.

Dr. Smollet raised a finger. "But I've found a way to make him talk," he said. "Just listen to me."

He motioned to the stools at the counter. The three of us took seats.

"It's simple, really," Dr. Smollet said. "It sounds more frightening than it is."

"What are you talking about?" Tara demanded.

"There's only one way to learn what Mr. Harvey knows," Dr. Smollet said. "We switch his brain with the brain of a live human."

Nicky and Tara both turned to me. "You mean *Max*?"

12

DR. SMOLLET NODDED. HE narrowed his eyes at me.

I slid off the stool. "Bye," I said. I started toward the door.

"Max, wait—!" Tara called. "Just let him finish."

I turned to Dr. Smollet. "You want to cut out our brains and switch them?" I cried. "Are you some kind of mad scientist? Like from a horror movie?"

I realized I was shouting. Normally, I'm a pretty quiet, shy guy. But I was trembling with fear. I wanted *out* of there!

"There is no cutting," Dr. Smollet said. "No surgery. Max, there is no danger at all. I promise you."

"Then how are you going to do it?" I asked. My voice cracked.

Dr. Smollet reached up to the cables that ran along the ceiling. He pulled down a set of headphones.

"I attach these to your heads. Then I allow the brain waves to flow freely between you and Mr. Harvey."

"Yeah, right," I said. "Then I'm going to pull off my head, turn it upside down, and fill it with M&M's!"

"I'm totally serious," Dr. Smollet said. "And I'm not crazy, Max. I know I can do this. When Mr. Harvey's brain waves are in your body, he will be able to speak."

"Hoo hoo," Mr. Harvey said. He jumped up onto the lab table and did a little dance.

"Max, with the help of your brain, tongue, and vocal system, Mr. Harvey will reveal everything he knows," Dr. Smollet said.

I jammed my hands into my pockets to stop them from shaking. I realized my whole body was trembling.

He wasn't serious about this.

He *couldn't* be serious!

"M-my brain?" I stammered. "Will my brain switch to his body? Will I be a *chimp*?"

"Hoo hoo." Mr. Harvey stomped along the lab table—and jumped into my lap. He gave me another toothy grin, raised both hands, and started playing with my face. Patting it and pulling at my cheeks.

"It will take only a few minutes," Dr. Smollet said. He tried to pull Mr. Harvey off me. But the chimp wrapped his arms around my waist and wouldn't let go.

Tara laughed. "He likes you, Max! I think he's in love!"

"He . . . he wants my *brain*!" I choked out.

"It won't even take half an hour," Dr. Smollet said. "I promise. No pain. You won't even feel it, Max. Mr. Harvey will reveal his secrets. Then I'll switch the brain waves back. It's totally safe. And so fast, you'll hardly realize it's happening at all."

I swallowed hard. Everyone was staring at me. Even Mr. Harvey.

"I . . . don't . . . think . . . so," I said. "In fact, read my lips: *No way!*"

I handed the chimp to Dr. Smollet. Then I headed for the door again. I expected Nicky and Tara to follow me. But when I turned back, they hadn't moved from their lab stools.

"Stop staring at me like that," I snapped. "What's your problem?"

Tara tugged at one earring. "It would mean an awful lot to Nicky and me," she said. She gave me this pleading look—big eyes and a sad frown.

"Look, guys—you're talking about my *brain*," I said softly. "I . . . I can't do it. I can't be a chimp. I don't even like bananas!"

"But Dr. Smollet says it's not dangerous," Nicky said. "Please, Max. If it could bring us back to life . . ."

47

"You'd do it for *us*—wouldn't you, Max?" Tara asked.

"Hoo hoo." Mr. Harvey tried to leap onto my chest. But Dr. Smollet held him back.

I turned to Dr. Smollet. "Okay, where are the hidden cameras?" I asked. "We're on *America's Funniest Home Videos* right now—aren't we?"

He shook his head. "No wacky videos," he said. "I've worked long and hard on this project. I owe Nicky and Tara's parents a lot. I hope I can repay them."

I squinted at him, studying his face. "Do you *swear* it's not dangerous?" I asked.

He raised his right hand. "I'm a scientist," he said. "I don't want to harm anyone. I just want to help the Roland family."

I turned to the chimp. He was hopping up and down now, grunting and scratching his stomach with his huge, hairy hands.

I didn't *want* my brain inside his head.

I liked my brain just where it was. It was nice and cozy right there in my head.

It was a good brain. In fact, the kids at school all call me Brainimon because I'm the smartest kid in class.

Did I want them to start calling me Chimpimon?

No way.

"I . . . I can't do this," I said. I avoided Nicky's

and Tara's eyes. I knew I was letting them down.
I knew they were *desperate* for any information.
Anything that could help them return to a nor-
mal life.

I raised my eyes. They were both watching
me. Both had eager, pleading expressions on their
faces.

"Well . . . maybe . . . ," I murmured.

"Hoo hoo!" Mr. Harvey cried, as if he understood.

"Max, no pressure," Dr. Smollet said. "I don't
want to rush you. I don't want you to do something against your will."

"Th-thanks," I said.

"I'll give you a week to think about it," he said.
"I'll come back for the three of you next Saturday."

He lifted Mr. Harvey into his arms. And then
he led the way out of the lab.

Near the door, I stopped and picked up Mr.
Harvey's red baseball cap. I slipped it onto my
head. *It fit perfectly!*

Was that a good omen?

Or a very bad omen?

"Oh, wow," I muttered. I tossed the cap across
the room and followed my friends down the long
white hall.

This, I told myself, is going to be the longest
week of my life!

i3

WAS THERE STILL TIME to perform for Ballantine?

I checked my watch. It was nearly three o'clock.

Dr. Smollet drove us into town and let us off across the street from Hocus Pocus. That's the name of the magic store.

To my surprise, I saw a long line of people waiting to get in. It stretched around the corner and down the block.

I crossed the street and hurried to get in line too. Guys were juggling duckpins and doing card tricks for each other. A tall bald guy was pulling egg after egg out of his mouth.

"You're still in time," Tara said. "That's so cool!"

I blinked. I was so excited about a chance to perform for Ballantine, I'd nearly forgotten Nicky and Tara were there.

I stepped in line behind a woman in a shiny black top hat and a tuxedo jacket. She was busy stuffing a mile-long chain of handkerchiefs into the jacket pocket.

"It's gonna be *hours* till you get in the store," Nicky said. "That'll give you time to chill and stop thinking about Dr. Smollet."

"Thanks for bringing it up again," I said. I sighed. "I can't believe how much you two have changed my life. My biggest problem used to be getting my hair to stay down!"

"It's *still* your biggest problem," Tara said. She tried to flatten my curly brown hair with the palm of her hand. But it bounced right back up.

"Oh, sure," I moaned. "Now I have to worry about having a chimp brain in my head!"

The woman in the top hat spun around. "Are you talking to me, young man?" she asked.

"Uh . . . no," I said. "I was talking to myself. Just rehearsing a magic trick."

"I think you'll be cute as a chimp," Tara teased.

"*You* look like a chimp!" I shouted.

The woman in the top hat gasped. "Young man, what is your problem?" she snapped. "How dare you talk to me like that?"

"You're getting yourself in trouble," Tara said.

"Just shut up!" I cried.

The top hat woman gasped again. "Someone needs to teach you some manners!" she shouted. "If you were *my* son, I'd slap you in the face!"

She flashed me an angry scowl and stomped away. The chain of handkerchiefs flew out of her pocket and trailed behind her.

"Well, that's *one* way to move up in line!" Nicky said.

"Can't you two disappear or something?" I said.

Tara slid her arm around my shoulders. "Come on, Maxie. Admit it. We've made your life exciting."

"Maybe I don't *want* an exciting life," I said.

"Then why are you in line?" the man ahead of me asked.

"I wasn't talking to you," I said.

He pulled an egg out of his mouth, then turned his back on me.

"Listen, guys, I can't do it," I said. "I can't switch brains with a chimp. I'm sorry. But I don't look good in red spandex shorts."

"Max, you heard what Dr. Smollet said," Nicky replied. "He said it will only last a few minutes."

"A few minutes is a long time!" I cried. "What if Mr. Harvey has fleas?"

Tara squeezed my hand. "You have to do it, Max," she said softly. "Don't you want my family to be alive again? Do you really want Nicky and me to be dead *for the rest of our lives*?"

"Please—go away," I said. "I have to think

about my card tricks now. I have to impress Ballantine."

Nicky and Tara vanished. The line moved up pretty quickly.

Finally, a man dressed in black stepped up to me. He had a badge around his neck, white with red letters: MAGIC STAFF. He put his hand on my shoulder.

"Okay, next victim. Kid, you can go in the store now."

Would Ballantine like my card tricks?

I took a deep breath. And stepped into the magic shop.

14

THE TINY STORE WAS jammed with people. Everyone wanted to get a glimpse of Ballantine the Nearly Amazing.

Magicians filled the aisles between the display cases of magic tricks. They were all talking at once. Talking about how their performances had gone and what Ballantine had said to them. Some looked happy. Some were shaking their heads sadly.

"Better luck next time," a chubby bald man said to another chubby bald man. He squeezed the other man's shoulder—and a pigeon flew out from under the guy's coat!

Weird crowd, huh?

I gazed around quickly. Was I the only kid?

Yes!

That has to be good, I told myself. At least Ballantine will notice me.

The line of magicians waiting to perform snaked around to the back room. I peeked ahead. I saw a small stage with a dark blue curtain behind it. A magician in a red cape stood on the stage doing a trick with three big, silvery rings.

And seated across from the stage on a tall chair that looked like a throne—Ballantine himself!

Several people huddled around Ballantine, including Mr. and Mrs. Hocus, the owners of Hocus Pocus. They all stared straight ahead in total silence, watching the magician do his ring trick.

"My two-year-old can do that trick!" a magician in line ahead of me whispered. A few people snickered at that.

"*Silence!*" a voice boomed through the store. Ballantine's voice. "We must give these performers every chance."

He stood up, and I got a better look at him. He was very lanky. He wore a glittery rhinestone turban on his head. He glowed in an aqua suit, very shiny and tight-fitting.

Ballantine's skin was deeply tanned. He had a narrow face with a thin black mustache. His eyelids drooped so low, I couldn't tell if his eyes were open. In fact, everything about him drooped. He had the saddest, droopiest expression I'd ever seen on a human.

No joke. He really did look as if his puppy had just died.

Of course, I'd seen videos of him. And I'd seen him on TV shows. And he always had that sad, hangdog look on his face. I wondered if anyone had ever seen Ballantine smile!

The line moved up. I started to feel nervous. It felt like a frog was jumping around in my stomach. I pulled out my deck of cards, and my hands were sweaty.

How am I going to do my tricks with sweaty hands? I asked myself. The frog leaped up to my throat.

I suddenly felt like turning around and running away. Ballantine was one of the most famous magicians in the world. Maybe the *universe*. What made me think I could impress him with my card tricks?

I wiped my hands on my jeans. I started to open the deck of cards and dropped them onto the floor. The cards spilled out around my feet.

My heart began to pound. I bent down and started to scoop them up. When I stood up again, Nicky and Tara were at my sides.

"Don't be nervous, Max," Tara said. "Nicky and I are going to help you."

"Huh? Help me?" I gasped.

I felt a tap on my shoulder. "You're next, kid," the man in black said. He gave me a little shove toward the stage.

15

NICKY AND TARA MOVED forward with me.

Ballantine was talking to the people around him. He was sipping coffee from a large white mug. He glanced at me, and his expression got even sadder.

"Piece of cake," Tara said. "Tap knuckles, Max, and let's show off a little!"

"I don't want to tap knuckles," I said.

Ballantine set down his coffee mug and stared at me. "You want to tap knuckles?"

"N-no," I said. "Just thinking out loud."

"Stop shaking like that, Max," Tara said. "Nicky and I are right here with you."

"Please! Go away!" I shouted.

Ballantine laughed. "Is this a comedy act?"

"No," I said. I raised the deck of cards.

Ballantine squinted at me from under his glittery turban. "What is your name, kid?"

Nicky whispered, "Tell him you're Max-o the Magnificent."

"I'm *not* Max-o the Magnificent!" I cried.

I heard people snicker.

"That's who you're *not*?" Ballantine asked. "You're confusing me. Who are you? And what planet do you come from?"

That got a big laugh from everyone in the room.

"Tell him you want to mystify his mind," Tara whispered.

"*Please* go away!" I begged Nicky and Tara.

Ballantine laughed. "This is a new approach," he told Mr. and Mrs. Hocus.

"The kid is kinda funny," Mr. Hocus said.

"Do you do any tricks, or do you just stand there and act weird?" Ballantine asked.

"I'm going to do some card tricks that I invented," I said.

"Card tricks are too dull," Nicky said.

"Yeah," Tara agreed. "Let's show him something more exciting."

"Please—let me do my card tricks," I begged.

Ballantine shrugged. "I'm not stopping you, kid."

"Let's do the Floating Wallet trick," Nicky said. "That's more fun."

I felt him pull my wallet from my jeans pocket. I made a grab for it. But Nicky raised it high over my head.

Ballantine and the others gasped.

They couldn't see Nicky. They just saw the wallet floating over my head.

I grabbed for it again. Nicky tossed it high to Tara.

Some people started to applaud. Ballantine actually opened his eyes all the way.

The wallet flew high over my head.

"I guess prices are going *up*!" I announced.

That got a big laugh.

Finally, I grabbed the wallet away from Nicky. I struggled to shove it back into my jeans pocket. "Let me do my card tricks," I said.

But Tara pulled the deck of cards from my hand and started tossing cards across the room to Nicky. He caught them and tossed them back to her.

I heard gasps around the room.

I ran frantically back and forth, trying to catch the cards. Nicky and Tara were ruining my act. Ruining my one chance with Ballantine.

The cards scattered across the floor. Ballantine's jaw dropped. He looked even more confused.

"Let's give him something to stare at," Tara said.

She and Nicky grabbed me by the armpits—and lifted me.

"Let me go!" I screamed.

They lifted me higher. I was floating nearly a foot off the floor.

Ballantine jumped to his feet. Everyone was chattering and gasping. "What do you call this trick?" Ballantine asked.

Nicky and Tara started to run. I looked as if I was flying across the room.

"Too . . . heavy . . . ," I heard Nicky groan.

"I'm losing him," Tara grunted. "Can't . . . hold . . . on."

"Nooo!" I let out a cry as they dropped me.

I fell hard on my face. Pain shot down my body.

I don't know how long I sprawled there, face-down, waiting for the pain to fade. When I stood up, I felt warm liquid oozing over my lips, down my chin.

A nosebleed. I had a fierce nosebleed.

My cards were scattered everywhere. The room had grown totally silent.

With a loud groan, I pulled myself to my feet. I didn't dare look at Ballantine.

My act was ruined.

I'd practiced for weeks. I knew my card tricks were good.

But it was all ruined—thanks to the two ghosts.

I'd never been so embarrassed in all my life. I

had made a total fool of myself—in front of one of my heroes.

With a sigh, holding one hand over my bleeding nose, I slumped toward the door.

"Come on," I muttered to Nicky and Tara. "Let's get out of here."

16

"WAIT! COME BACK!" **A** voice boomed.

I turned to see Ballantine waving to me.

Was I seeing things? Did he actually have a smile on his face?

"Wonderful," he said. "What's your name?"

"Max Doyle," I said. Mrs. Hocus handed me a wad of Kleenex. I pressed it against my bleeding nose.

"That's a very funny act you do," Ballantine said. He pulled off his turban and scratched his thick, curly white hair. "I know magicians don't tell their secrets. But you will have to come back, Max, and tell me how you do that floating trick."

"C-come back?" I stammered.

He nodded. "Yes. Come back next Saturday. You have passed the audition. You will go on to the next round."

He turned to Mr. Hocus. "Write down his name. Max Doyle. I definitely want to see him next week."

"Thank you," I said.

"Is that blood real? Or is it trick blood?" Ballantine asked.

"Uh . . . trick blood," I said. "All part of the act."

Back in my room, I sprawled on my back on the bed. I stared up at the ceiling, taking deep breaths. Thinking hard about Ballantine and everything that had happened at the magic store.

When Nicky and Tara appeared at the side of the bed, I wasn't happy to see them.

"I need time to think," I said. "I need peace and quiet. Can you take a hint?"

"No, we can't," Tara said, sitting down next to me. She gave me several soft face slaps. "Snap out of it, Maxie."

"Why won't you leave me alone?" I begged.

"Because we haven't heard you say thank you yet," Nicky replied, dropping down beside his sister.

"Thank you?" I cried, sitting up. "Thank you for *what*?"

"For making your act so good, Ballantine wants you to come back," Tara said.

"You're joking, right?" I said. "You didn't make my act good. You made my act a *disaster*! And—and—"

My nose started to bleed again. I grabbed a wad of tissues and pressed them against my face.

"We help each other," Tara insisted. "Admit it, Max. Nicky and I helped you. And next Saturday . . . you'll help us."

"Huh?" I jumped out of bed. "You mean switch brains with a monkey? You're crazy! You—"

The front doorbell rang. I was the only one home. "Go away," I told Nicky and Tara. "Maybe I do owe you thanks for what happened in the magic store. But *no way* will I switch brains with that chimp. Do you hear me? No way!"

"Is that a *maybe*?" Tara asked.

She and Nicky vanished. The doorbell chimed again. I ran downstairs and pulled open the front door.

"Traci!" I gasped.

There stood Traci Wayne in all her golden beauty. Traci Wayne, the coolest, prettiest, most awesome girl at Jefferson Elementary. Traci Wayne—standing on my front stoop!

What did I do to deserve such amazing luck?

Yes, I admit I have a crush on Traci. I mean, I think it may be true love. Whenever I see her, my toes curl up, so it takes me hours to pull my shoes off.

My face turns bright red. I start breathing through my mouth, making *hee-haw* sounds. And I get all tongue-tied and say everything backward.

Is that true love? Or is it some kind of weird disease?

I stared at Traci. Her blond hair ruffled behind her in the wind. Her olive-colored eyes locked on mine.

"Goodbye," I said. "I mean, hello. Hee-haw. Hee-haw."

"Hi, Max," she said. She glanced around. "Can I come inside? I don't want my friends to see me at your house. That would be so uncool."

"Hee-haw. I understand," I said. I moved away so she could step inside.

She hurried in and shut the door behind her.

She was wearing a pale blue sweater and jeans. I glanced down and saw that my nose had dripped a couple of red spots onto her white tennis sneakers.

She looked down too. "Oh, what's that on my new shoes?" she asked.

"Hee-haw. It's blood," I said.

"Ew. Blood?"

I tried to sound in control. I punched my fist in the air. "A bloody nose," I said. "I got into a fight."

Traci squinted at me. "You? Brainimon? In a fight?"

"Ha, ha," I said. "I don't want to brag. But you should have seen the *other* guy!"

She sneered at me. "What *really* happened? You fell on your face?"

"Kind of," I said.

She glanced at the front window. "No one can see me in here, right?"

"Right," I said. "What's down, Traci? I mean, what's *up*?"

"Listen, Max. My icky cousin Stella is having a drippy, boring party. Her friends are all nerds and geeks. But my mom is making me go."

I suddenly started panting like an overheated dog. "Yeah?"

"I need to bring someone with me," Traci said. "But I don't want to invite any of my cool friends. Cuz they'd hate it. They'd hate it cuz it's going to be the *worst,* most geeky, most yuck-all party in history."

"Cool," I said. "I mean, hee-haw."

"I can't think of anyone else in school uncool enough to go to this party," Traci said. "Except for you, Max. So how about it?"

With a loud sigh, I fell back against the wall. Dazed. Totally dazed.

The invitation of a *lifetime*!

Traci Wayne was actually inviting me to a party!

"Sweet!" I said. "I mean, awesome!"

"We'll go in separate cars," Traci said. "I don't want my friends to know I went to a party with you."

"That's cool," I said. "I mean, okay."

"Okay. See you Saturday," Traci said. She glanced around tensely. "Can I go out the back door? I don't want anyone to see that I was here."

"No problem," I said. "Hee-haw. See you Saturday."

I watched her run out the back door. She took off across the backyard running full speed and didn't look back.

My luck is definitely changing! I told myself.

Ballantine the Nearly Amazing invited me back to perform for a second week. And Traci Wayne invited me to a party.

Was this the luckiest day of my life?

Or was it the *last* happy Saturday I would ever have?

17

THE WEEK DRAGGED BY. I felt like I was moving in slow motion.

Nicky and Tara kept begging me to go with them to Dr. Smollet's lab Saturday morning. But I tried to shove that thought out of my mind.

All I could think about was performing magic tricks for Ballantine and going to Traci's cousin's party.

Thursday after school, I went home with Aaron. I wanted to show him the tricks I planned to do for Ballantine.

Aaron looked even weirder than usual. That's because he still had the cell phone glued to his ear.

"It's kinda nice for making calls," he said as we climbed the stairs to his room. "I never have to look for the phone. But it's hard to power up. I have to lean my head close to the charger and hold it there for about an hour."

"How long are you going to keep it there?" I asked.

Aaron shrugged. "My doctor tried everything

68

to remove it. But he couldn't do it. He called the glue company to send someone to look at me. Maybe they can help."

I set up my tricks on Aaron's desk. He sat down on his bed to watch.

"Is that a new Jennifer Garner poster?" I asked, pointing to the wall behind his bed. Aaron had taped posters and pictures over the entire wall.

"Yeah," Aaron said. "Check it out."

I stepped up to the poster. It was a scene from the first season of *Alias*. Jennifer Garner's hair was blowing behind her. She had a shiny gun in her hand.

"Hey!" I read the handwriting near the bottom. It was a message written in blue ink: To Aaron, Love always—Jennifer.

"Wow!" I cried, turning to Aaron. "She signed this for you?"

He shook his head. "No. I wrote that. Cool, huh?"

"Yeah. Sure," I said. I walked back to the desk. "Here's a new trick. I made it up just for Ballantine."

I held up two drinking glasses. "The Amazing Moving Water Trick!" I announced. "Watch carefully."

The glass on the left was filled with water. I held a red handkerchief in front of the glasses, hiding them from view.

"The water moves in mysterious ways!" I boomed in my loud magician's voice. I whipped the handkerchief away—and both glasses were now half full.

"Awesome," Aaron said. "The water really did move."

"Keep watching," I said. I hid the glasses behind the handkerchief. "Move, water!" I shouted. I pulled the handkerchief away—and all the water was now in the second glass.

"Awesome!" Aaron repeated. He clapped his hands. "How do you do that?"

"Wait. I'm not finished," I said. I lowered the handkerchief again and said some magic words. This time, both glasses were empty. The water had disappeared.

Aaron jumped to his feet. "That is way cool!" he exclaimed. He slapped me on the back. I staggered into the desk, and both glasses started to tumble off.

Luckily, I made a great catch and grabbed them before they fell.

"Ballantine will go ape for that trick!" Aaron said.

"Please don't mention monkeys," I begged.

He stared at me. "Huh? Excuse me?"

"Never mind," I said.

"Did you know I'm allergic to monkeys?" Aaron asked.

"I have some more tricks," I said.

Aaron picked up the two water glasses. "Bet I can do the water trick," he said. He raised the two glasses to his face and studied them.

I laughed. "Since when are you into magic?" I asked.

I heard a noise outside the bedroom window. Someone was shouting out there.

I ran to the window, stuck my head out, and glanced around. I heard more shouts. Then I saw some kids in the yard across the street.

The Wilbur brothers. They were beating up a little kid. He was screaming for help.

I watched Billy Wilbur rip the boy's shirt up the back. Willy Wilbur held the kid down and gave his head a hard knuckle rub.

"Hey! The Wilbur brothers are beating up a kid across the street!" I called to Aaron.

"So what else is new?" Aaron replied. "Dude, they beat that kid up every afternoon. It's their after-school activity."

I watched for a few more seconds. The little kid kicked Willy in the leg, then ran away.

A happy ending.

When I turned back to Aaron, he had a worried look on his face.

"Uh . . . Max? I'm in a little trouble here," he said. He raised his hands. Both hands were stuck inside the water glasses.

"Take them off. That's not how you do the water trick," I told him.

"I . . . can't get them off," Aaron said. He held his hands out to me. "Help me, okay? *Pull!*"

I tried pulling the glass off his left hand. Then the right. I pulled as hard as I could. But I had to be careful. I didn't want to break the glass.

I tried twisting them off. Then I tried pushing and pulling.

No way.

Those glasses were stuck on tight.

"I'm not happy about this," Aaron said, shaking his head. The cell phone on his ear shook too.

I had to laugh. He had a phone stuck to his ear and two glasses stuck to his hands.

"I know what we can do," Aaron said. "My tool kit is under the bed. Get the hammer and smash the glasses."

I frowned at him. "I don't *think* so!" I said. "I need these glasses. They're trick glasses. They make it look like there's water inside. But there's no water in this trick."

"Come on, Max. Use the hammer," Aaron begged. "I'm desperate here."

"No way," I said. "Your hands will be cut. You'll bleed all over the place."

That's when Aaron's mom burst into the room. Her mouth dropped open when she saw the glasses stuck on Aaron's hands.

"I don't *believe* this!" she screamed. "This isn't happening."

Aaron nodded. He had both hands raised in front of him. "Yes it is," he muttered.

"I have to take you to the emergency room *again*?" his mom cried.

"It's Max's fault!" Aaron exclaimed. "It's his magic trick. He said I should do it."

"No, wait—!" I cried. "That's not true. I—"

"Aaron, you're grounded for *another* lifetime!" his mom shouted.

Then she turned to me. "You made Aaron do this? When I get back from the hospital, I'm calling your mom. She should ground you, too!"

My heart pounded as I watched her drag Aaron to the car. Aaron turned and waved to me, his hands trapped inside the glasses.

The door shut behind him. The car backed down the driveway.

I watched until it disappeared down the street.

"Hey, I can't be grounded!" I called after them. "Saturday is going to be the biggest day of my life!"

18

FRIDAY AFTER SCHOOL, TRACI pulled me into the teachers' parking lot. It was a warm, breezy day. The wind kept blowing her blond hair into her face. She kept brushing it back with one hand, glancing around, making sure none of her cool friends saw her talking to me.

She wore an olive green sweater that matched her eyes. And olive cargo pants that matched the sweater that matched her eyes.

Keep it together, Max, I told myself. But I realized I was already making that *hee-haw* sound I've been making lately whenever she comes near me.

"Remember about the party tomorrow evening?" she asked.

"Hee-haw," I said. "You and I—"

"Remember we're going in separate cars?" she said. "And don't talk to me too much at the party. Just in case someone cool shows up."

"Hee-haw," I said. "No problem."

"And promise you won't embarrass me in any

74

way," Traci said. "These kids are all geeks and freaks. But I still don't want to be embarrassed."

"Hee-haw," I said. "Hee-haw."

Traci brushed back her hair. Then she handed me a flashlight.

"What's this for?" I asked.

"It's a flashlight party," she said, rolling her eyes. "My cousin's house is going to be totally dark. And you need a flashlight to get into the party."

"Cool!" I said.

"No, it's totally *un*cool," Traci replied. "I told you my cousin Stella is a drip."

She hurried away.

I staggered back against one of the cars. I couldn't believe it! I was going to a flashlight party with Traci Wayne! Of course, we wouldn't talk to each other or anything. But how *exciting* was this?

"Hee-haw. Hee-haw."

Why did I keep making that sound? Did it mean true love?

I started to walk home. The wind blew at my back. I felt as if I could lift off the ground and float home.

I felt a strong puff of air. At first I thought it was just a gust of wind. Then I realized Nicky and Tara were at my sides.

"Maxie, why are you grinning like that?" Tara asked.

I stared at her. "Don't know," I said. "Just grinning."

"Are you grinning because you decided to be a nice guy and help Tara and me on Saturday?" Nicky asked.

I stopped walking. We were at the corner of Powell and Bleek, my street. The wind suddenly picked up. I shivered. It had been warm, but now the breeze felt cold.

Gray clouds floated close overhead.

"Listen, guys," I said quietly. "I know how badly you want me to do that chimp thing for you. I've been thinking and thinking about it all week."

"And?" Tara demanded.

I shook my head. "I can't do it. It's just too scary. And too dangerous."

They both groaned. Tara took my arm. "Come on, Max," she said. "You promised you'd help us, remember? When we first came to your house?"

"I never promised I'd switch my brain with an animal brain," I said. "Look, guys, you know I'm your friend. You know I want to help you. But—"

I didn't finish. The wind howled. A powerful gust shook the trees all around. Darkness fell, as if the clouds had dropped over us.

The sky was suddenly black as night.

Another howl. Like a wild, angry animal.

The tree leaves were all shaking now. The tree limbs, too. It grew even darker. The wind swirled around me.

"What's up with this?" I cried.

I staggered back as a creature lurched toward us. Out of the blackness, it shot forward.

I saw its yellow eyes first. Angry yellow eyes.

Then I saw its black panther head. Its curved teeth bared. Its angry expression.

A creature on two legs. Huge and howling. Its eyes fierce as fire.

"Noooooo!" A shriek of horror escaped my throat.

We started to run. All three of us. My two ghost friends and me, bent low into the howling, swirling wind. Struggling to run, to fight the wind and the darkness—and to flee this thing!

I heard the hard thumps and bumps of its heavy paws on the pavement. A gust of hot wind—its *breath* on the back of my neck!

What was it?

Some creature of darkness! Yellow-eyed and angry.

And loping after us. Taking its time. Howling out its fury.

The darkness grew deeper. Colder.

Hard to breathe. My leg muscles cramping. Hard to move.

And then I saw the creature grab them.

It grabbed Nicky and Tara in its front paws. Long, curved ivory talons closed around my friends.

The creature bent low, holding the two ghosts high in front of it—and sprang away. Leaped into the darkness on two powerful legs, still howling, those headlight eyes still prowling.

"Help us! Max—help us!"

I heard their terrified cries in the howl of the wind.

19

I FROZE.

The wind blew harder, pushing me back, shoving me away from the creature.

The huge animal tossed back its head and sent a long howl up to the dark sky. I could see Nicky and Tara gripped in its talons, squirming and thrashing, struggling to free themselves.

"Help us! Max!"

"Max! Help!"

What could I do?

I gaped at the horrifying creature—like a monstrous black panther, bounding on its hind legs. As it turned away from me, I saw its tail, curled up on its back like a long black snake!

"Help us! Max—do something!"

My whole body trembled, violent shudder after shudder. The flashlight nearly slid from my hand.

The flashlight!

An idea burst into my mind. A desperate idea. But maybe . . . just maybe . . .

79

I gripped the flashlight tightly. I raised it to my waist and pointed it at the howling creature.

I remembered the evil ghost Phears, who had wanted to destroy Nicky and Tara.

I remembered the first time Phears came after me.

Bright car headlights had scared him away.

Phears couldn't stand bright light. It made him helpless. It burned his ghostly skin like fire.

Would the light from this flashlight have the same effect on this creature?

Could I surprise the big animal long enough for Nicky and Tara to escape?

My hand shook so hard, the flashlight again started to slide out. I gripped it in both hands.

The creature leaped over a hedge and disappeared into the darkness on the other side.

"No!" I cried out.

I couldn't let it get away. Lowering my head, I ran full force into the hedge. Its prickly branches scratched my hands and face. But I pushed straight through to the other side.

The creature had its back to me. Its snakelike tail curled and uncurled on its furry back.

Ducking against the onrushing wind, I ran hard to catch up with the monster. Holding my friends tightly in front of itself. Tilting its head back, howling into the rush of wind.

Well, I'm going to give you something to howl about! I thought.

I raised the flashlight. Aimed it at the creature's broad back.

And clicked it on. Clicked it hard.

Nothing happened.

Nothing.

No light. No light at all.

20

I SHOOK THE FLASHLIGHT.

I clicked it again.

No. The light didn't flash on.

I clicked it again. Again. My heart pounding each time.

It was dead. The flashlight was dead.

The creature was escaping with my friends.

Their screams had stopped. Had he strangled them with those long, curved talons?

The wind swirled around me as I chased the monster, squeezing the flashlight in both hands. Clicking it helplessly again and again.

I didn't see the rock at the side of a driveway. With a loud cry, I stumbled over it and went sprawling onto my stomach on the ground.

The flashlight hit the pavement. Bounced hard.

And a beam of bright white light shot out of it.

Yes! It was working now!

I dove for it. Grabbed it up. Struggled to my feet.

Gasping for breath, I ran after the howling creature. I raised the flashlight. Aimed the beam of light into the creature's black, furry back.

The monster stopped. It raised its head—and opened its mouth in an angry roar.

I gasped as it whirled around to face me.

Holding the flashlight in both hands, I raised the beam of light to the panther creature's face.

It howled in pain. Raised its front paws to shield its eyes from the light.

Nicky and Tara dropped free. Toppled to the ground.

The light beam trembled. But I kept it on the monster's face.

It let out another roar, softer this time. The creature tossed its head back and shook its paws as if trying to wave the light beam away.

I expected it to turn and run. But instead, it dropped to its knees, uttering low whimpers as it sank to the ground.

I lowered the light beam. Kept it focused on the creature's head.

And watched the monster sink into the grass and start to dissolve.

As I stared in shock, it melted into a lumpy black puddle. A round black stain on the grass.

Finally, my whole body shaking, I lowered the light beam. I clicked off the flashlight and ran to Nicky and Tara.

They had climbed to their feet and were gazing around as if in a daze.

"It . . . it's gone!" Nicky cried.

Tara pulled off her red hat and shook out her dark hair. "Whoa . . . Max . . . you . . . you did it!"

Nicky and Tara were fading in and out of view. I knew that their fright had drained a lot of their energy. I could see right through them!

The darkness lifted as suddenly as it had come. And the wind stopped howling and swirling. I could see stars in the evening sky and a bright full moon.

I breathed a long sigh of relief.

Nicky tapped knuckles with me. "Way to go, dude," he said.

Tara was still shaking her head. She brushed tears off her cheeks. "See, Max?" she said in a whisper. "There are so many ghosts and evil creatures out there. So many evil creatures who are our enemies because of the work Mom and Dad did."

She grabbed my arm. She was so faint, I could barely feel it. "Nicky and I aren't safe," she said. "We're never safe. And we won't be safe until we know the truth—until we know what happened to us and how we can return to life."

She faded even more. I could barely see the two of them now. They weren't even shadows. They were wisps of faint color.

"You saw what happened just now. You've got to help us, Max," Nicky whispered. "You've *got* to!"

I pictured the evil panther creature. I pictured Nicky and Tara trapped in its long claws. My friends . . . my *best* friends being carried away . . .

I swallowed. "Okay," I said. "I'll do it. I'll switch brains with the monkey."

21

SATURDAY MORNING I WOKE up early. I stared at myself in the dresser mirror. "Max, this could be the best or worst day of your life," I told my reflection.

The reflection stared back at me and didn't reply.

What a day I had planned. First I'd switch brains with a chimpanzee. Then I'd perform magic in front of one of the world's greatest magicians. Then I'd go to a party with Traci Wayne.

With a day like that, it's no wonder I was talking to myself!

A few hours later, Dr. Smollet met Nicky, Tara, and me at the place where we'd first met and drove us to his lab. He seemed very cheerful. He kept talking about what a great day this would be for Nicky and Tara.

I slumped in the backseat and hardly said a word. I wanted to shove open the car door and run as far as I could.

But I'd made a promise to my friends. And I was going to grit my teeth and keep my promise.

This will all be over soon, I told myself. I forced myself to think about Ballantine and the magic tricks I had planned to show him.

As we walked through the long white halls of the lab, I heard the distant shrieks and wails of animals again. Their cages were hidden away.

Dr. Smollet led us to the same room as before. On the long table, a row of computer monitors blinked and glowed. Machines hummed against the wall.

Two tall stools had been set near the computer table. Dr. Smollet motioned for me to sit on one of them.

My legs were trembling so hard, I had trouble climbing onto the stool.

Dr. Smollet put his hand on my shoulder. "Don't worry, Max," he said softly. "You'll be fine. You'll see."

He typed for a few moments on the nearest keyboard. Then he hurried away to bring in Mr. Harvey.

Nicky and Tara had been admiring all the computers. When Dr. Smollet left the room, they rushed over to me.

"This is so awesome of you," Tara said. "I can't believe you're doing this for us."

"I can't either," I muttered.

"We're gonna owe you—big-time," Nicky said.

"Tell you the *first* thing we're gonna do for

you," Tara said. "We're gonna stay away from the magic store. Nicky and I are not going to help you with your act."

"Oh, thank you!" I cried. "That's the best news I've heard all day. And what *else* are you going to do for me?"

They didn't have a chance to answer. Dr. Smollet returned, leading the chimpanzee. "Mr. Harvey is ready to go," he said. He gave the chimp a gentle head rub.

A big, toothy grin spread over Mr. Harvey's face.

Dr. Smollet sat Mr. Harvey on the stool next to me. The chimp started to chatter and hop up and down. He reached out a big hand and mussed my hair.

"Settle down, Mr. Harvey," Dr. Smollet scolded. "I mean it. Settle down."

The chimp seemed to understand. He stopped chattering and dropped limply onto the stool.

"Mr. Harvey was here the day Phears did his dirty work," Dr. Smollet said to Nicky and Tara. "Once the chimp's brain waves are inside Max, he'll be able to tell us everything he saw."

He turned to me. "It won't take long," he said. "As soon as we learn what Mr. Harvey knows, I'll switch the brain waves back. And you'll be back to normal, Max."

I shoved my hands in my pockets to stop them

from shaking. I don't think I'd ever been this terrified in my life.

The chimp grinned at me, stuck out his tongue, and made a spitting noise.

"Uh . . . I'm sorry," I said. "I can't do this. I just remembered something I forgot to do."

"Max, what did you forget?" Tara asked.

"I forgot to leave!"

Dr. Smollet smiled. "Funny," he muttered. He slipped a pair of headphones over my head. I saw that they were attached to a maze of wires that ran into the computers.

"Max, don't be so nervous," he said. "I'm a doctor, remember?"

He turned and put another pair of headphones on the chimp's head. Mr. Harvey made a spitting noise at Dr. Smollet.

"If I start spitting like that, just smack me!" I said.

I was trying to make a joke. But everyone was too tense to laugh.

"Ready for the brain waves transfer," Dr. Smollet said.

He patted me on the shoulder. "Don't look so worried, Max," he said. "You won't feel a thing. . . ."

22

MY MOUTH SUDDENLY FELT dry as cotton. I couldn't swallow. I realized I was breathing hard, gasping for breath even though I was sitting still.

Mr. Harvey sat on the stool beside me. He held on to the headphones and bounced gently up and down.

Dr. Smollet began typing frantically on a computer keyboard. "Max, watch the monitor!" he shouted.

His voice was muffled because of the headphones I was wearing.

Nicky and Tara stepped up beside me. "This is totally awesome of you," Tara said. "I repeat. We'll owe you big-time."

"Yes, you will," I agreed.

On the monitor screen, I saw my profile and the chimp's profile. Leaning over the keyboard, Dr. Smollet kept typing.

I felt a buzzing in my head. Soft at first, then louder.

On the screen, my head and the chimp's head slid closer together.

The headphones began to vibrate. I reached my hands up and pressed against them. The buzz increased to a roar.

Nicky and Tara held me by the shoulders. The three of us stared at the monitor as my head and the chimp's head moved closer . . . closer together . . . closer . . .

Until Mr. Harvey's head covered mine.

I felt a whoosh of wind, as if someone had blown a puff of air inside my head.

It lasted only a second. A strange, frightening feeling that made my whole body shudder.

I gripped the headphones as if holding on to a lifeboat. And suddenly, I felt as if I was underwater. The air seemed to ripple like water. And I felt light, floating.

The monitor screen blurred. The white lab walls gleamed brighter and brighter until they washed everything else from my sight.

I blinked—and everything slowly drifted back into focus.

"Max? Are you okay?"

I could hear Tara's voice. But it sounded very far away.

"Max? Max?"

I blinked a few more times. Then I glanced

around, struggling to see clearly, my head still buzzing.

Mr. Harvey hadn't moved from the stool next to me. He still gripped his headphones and bounced up and down. Dr. Smollet was typing on his keyboard. Nicky and Tara stood next to me, their faces creased with worry.

I stuck my tongue out and made a loud spitting noise at them.

Oh no! *Why did I do that?*

"Sorry," I said. I tugged the headphones off.

"Max? How do you feel?" Dr. Smollet asked. He stepped over to my stool and took the headphones from me. "Are you okay?"

"I guess," I said. "I don't feel very different."

"Oh, thank goodness!" Tara cried.

"Hoo hoo hoo," I said.

Huh? Monkey noises?

Dr. Smollet smiled and nodded. "I think the transfer is working," he said.

"I still feel like me," I said. "I don't really feel hoo hoo hoo very different."

I tested my memory. I remembered my name . . . my address . . . my phone number.

Yes! I was still Max Doyle.

The brains didn't switch. I was still *me*!

I suddenly thought about lunch. Would there be a banana?

Dr. Smollet kept smiling at me. "Success! I'm

very pleased," he said. "It will take a short while for the chimp's brain to settle into Max's brain. But when it does—"

"Hoo hoooo," I said, hopping up and down on the tall stool. "Hoo hoo hooo."

"When the brain settles down," Dr. Smollet continued, "Mr. Harvey will be able to tell us—through Max—everything he saw."

"Hoo," I said, nodding. I reached out one hand and worked at removing a piece of fuzz from Tara's shirt.

"Max, do you feel totally weird?" Nicky asked.

I hopped up and down. "Hoo hoo," I said. "Yeah. Kinda weird. It's like there's someone else in here with me."

Dr. Smollet picked up the chimp. "Mr. Harvey seems a little dazed," he said. "I'm going to take him to the kitchen over there and give him something to eat."

He turned and started walking toward a white door at the far end of the lab. Mr. Harvey waved to us over Dr. Smollet's shoulder.

"When I come back, we'll question Max," Dr. Smollet said. "At last, you two kids will have some answers!"

He and the chimp disappeared into the kitchen.

Nicky and Tara had big grins on their faces. They were practically hopping up and down too.

"Max, this is so *awesome*!" Tara cried. "You're going to tell us what happened to our family. And maybe you can tell us how to be alive again!"

"Thanks, dude!" Nicky said. He slapped me a high five.

"Wish Mom and Dad were here," Tara said.

"Hoo hoo," I replied. I suddenly wanted to scratch my chest.

I struggled to think clearly. "You know, I still hoo hoo feel like me," I said. My voice came out scratchy and high. "And I still think like me," I told them. "But . . . I want a banana really badly."

Nicky and Tara laughed. They thought I was joking.

I shut my eyes for a moment and thought really hard.

Was the chimp's brain really inside mine? If so, why did I still think like me?

Yes, I was making chimp sounds. And yes, I had some chimp feelings.

But what about the chimp memories? What about the things Mr. Harvey was supposed to reveal to Nicky and Tara? Were those memories inside my head?

"Max, why are your eyes closed?" Nicky asked.

"What is it?" Tara demanded. "Are you okay? What are you thinking about?"

Good question.

I was thinking about bananas. And about scratching myself.

But *what else?*

Where were the important chimp memories?

Where was the important information?

"Uh-oh," I murmured. A wave of dread swept over me, making me feel heavy and cold.

"Hoo hoo," I said. "Something is wrong, guys. Something is *terribly* wrong."

23

THEY STARED AT ME with their mouths open.

I struggled to think clearly. If only I had a banana. Or maybe some grapes.

I suddenly had to go to the bathroom. Should I do it in my pants?

"Hoo hoo," I said.

I shook my head hard. No time for monkey talk. I had to tell Nicky and Tara what I was thinking.

"Listen, guys," I said in my scratchy voice. "Something is very wrong. Hoo hoo. The chimp brain is inside me. I can hoo hoo feel it."

"Yes?" Tara asked. "And?"

I reached up to her hair and started to work my fingers through it, grooming her, searching for fleas. She pulled my arm away gently. "Max, what are you trying to say?"

"The chimp brain is *empty*!" I cried. I started hopping furiously up and down. "Hoo hoo!"

"I—I don't understand," Nicky said. "What do you mean?"

"Give him a chance," Tara scolded her brother. "He's part chimp. It takes him time to get the words out."

I took a deep breath. "The brain is empty," I said, speaking slowly, forcing myself to concentrate. "It doesn't have any memories. There are no memories of you or your family."

"No way!" Tara cried. "You're just not thinking right, Max."

"There's nothing to think about," I said. "Hoo hoo hoo. I want a banana really badly. That's my only thought. Don't you see? Something is wrong. I have chimp thoughts—but no memories at all!"

I jumped down from the stool. I started toward the kitchen.

"Where are you going?" Tara cried. She and Nicky hurried after me.

I was lumbering from side to side, like a chimp.

"Don't panic, Max," Tara said. "Dr. Smollet will be able to get the memories from your brain. You have to wait for him."

"Hoo hoo," I said. "There's something weird going on."

I wobbled across the lab to the kitchen. Nicky and Tara ran close behind me.

I pulled open the door and we stepped inside.

No one there. An empty room.

And it wasn't a kitchen. It was an empty closet. With an open door at the other end.

"Dr. Smollet!" Nicky and Tara both shouted. "Dr. Smollet! Where are you?"

No answer.

All I could hear were the shrieks and cries of the lab animals far down the hall.

"Dr. Smollet? Dr. Smollet?"

We ran up and down the long halls, searching for him, shouting his name.

No answer.

"Hoo hoo," I said, hopping up and down angrily. "He and Mr. Harvey have run away!"

24

THE WORDS MADE ME dizzy. I sank onto the floor. I shook my head sadly.

"He . . . he took my brain," I whispered. "I . . . I'm half chimpanzee!"

Nicky and Tara dropped down beside me. "We'll find him," Tara said. "Don't worry, Max. We'll search the whole town if we have to."

"We'll get the rest of your brain back," Nicky said.

I felt sick. My stomach tightened into a knot. I didn't even want a banana anymore.

My brain. Part of my brain was inside that chimp. And part of his brain was inside me.

I didn't understand. Was it some kind of evil trick?

What if we never saw Dr. Smollet again? Would I be forced to spend the rest of my life as Max the Incredible Monkey Boy?

"No," I murmured. "No, no, no. Hoo hoo. This can't be happening to me."

I glanced at my watch. "I'm late!" I cried,

99

jumping up. "I'm late for my tryout with Ballantine!"

Nicky and Tara helped me up. "We'll get you to the audition," Tara said. "Don't worry."

"Hoooo," I said. I started picking at one of Tara's ears. Why couldn't I keep my hands off her head?

"I'm half chimp," I wailed. "How can I do my tricks?"

"Just act like everything is okay," Nicky said. "I'll bet no one even notices."

"Yeah, right," I said, rolling my eyes. "Halfway through my tricks, I'll start picking through Ballantine's hair!"

"He'll think it's part of the act," Tara said.

We walked down the long white halls. I could hear animals shrieking and crying on all sides. I wanted to sit down and cry too.

My brain. My beautiful, awesome brain was half chimp.

Nicky and Tara shouted Dr. Smollet's name all the way down the hall again.

Still no reply.

The front door stood wide open. Dr. Smollet and Mr. Harvey must have run out—in a very big hurry to get away.

But why?

Why run off and leave me like this?

"Go to the magic store and do your best," Tara

said. "Nicky and I will search this whole town. We won't give up until we find Dr. Smollet and that chimp. We'll get your brain back, Max. I promise."

"Yes, we both promise," Nicky said.

Why didn't their promise cheer me up?

I had to go home to get my magic kit. We climbed onto the Miller Street bus and walked all the way to the back.

"Hoo hoo," I said, shaking my head sadly.

Nicky and Tara sat down with their heads lowered, their hands clasped tightly in their laps. All three of us felt sick with worry. We didn't feel like talking.

A few blocks later, the driver suddenly stopped the bus. He climbed out of his seat and walked to the back. "Young man," he called. "Would you please stop swinging on the poles?"

Oops.

"Sorry," I muttered. I let go of the pole and dropped down beside Nicky and Tara. I didn't even realize I was swinging.

"Hoo hoo hoo," I said.

The driver stared at me for a long time. "Do you kids think you're funny?" he snarled.

"Hoo," I said.

"You know who," he snapped. "You, that's who."

"Hoo," I said.

Shaking his head, he walked back to the front

and started the bus up. I wanted to swing some more. But Nicky and Tara held me down.

"You'll be okay, Max," Tara said softly. "I promise. You'll be perfectly okay."

Of course she was wrong.

25

MOM DROVE ME TO the magic store. I sat beside her and stared straight ahead. I gripped my magic kit tightly in my lap.

"You're very quiet today," Mom said.

"Hoo," I replied.

"Who? You!" She laughed. "Are you worried about the famous magician?"

"Hoo," I said.

"You know. Ballantine," she replied.

"I'm a little tense," I managed to say. I put my lips together and made a loud, juicy spitting noise.

"After your tryout, I'll drive you straight to Traci's party," Mom said.

I made another spitting noise.

"The party won't be that bad," Mom said, pulling into a parking space. "I thought you had a crush on Traci Wayne."

"Hoo," I said.

"Ha, ha. Very funny," Mom replied, rolling her eyes. "You're in a very weird mood."

Well, yeah, Mom. You see, I've never been half chimpanzee before!

That's what I wanted to say. But of course I didn't.

I thanked her for the ride and climbed out of the car. Again, there was a big crowd around the magic store. The line of magicians stretched down the block. I wobbled my way to the back of the line.

Luckily, I had packed a couple of bananas and a few tangerines in my magic kit to keep up my energy. The woman in front of me had long red hair. I wanted to groom it for her. But somehow I managed to keep my hands to myself.

The line moved up slowly.

I couldn't help myself. I hopped up and down and shouted, "Hoo hoo hoo!"

The red-haired magician spun around. "What's your problem, kid?" she asked.

I shrugged. "Just warming up my voice," I said. I picked a piece of lint off her poncho. Then I pulled back my lips and flashed her a toothy grin.

She rolled her eyes and spun back around.

Finally, my turn came to perform for Ballantine the Nearly Amazing. He sat on his tall chair, with Mr. and Mrs. Hocus at his sides. Today he was dressed all in black—black trousers, a black turtleneck, and a black turban on his head.

"Hello, Max. Nice to see you back," he boomed in his deep voice.

He remembered me!

I climbed onto the little stage and took a bow. I'd brought a new trick with me because I couldn't do the drinking glass trick. Aaron's doctor had to break the glasses to get them off his hands.

I set a top hat upside down on the table on the stage. Then I raised a pitcher of water over the hat. "Hoo hoo. The Pitcher of Endless Disappearing Water!" I announced.

The idea was that I would pour the pitcher of water into the hat. The pitcher would keep pouring and pouring. It would never empty. And when I picked up the hat, it would be totally dry. No water.

It wasn't a hard trick. I'd practiced it hundreds of times.

But as I raised the pitcher, I suddenly got a better idea. I decided to stand on my head and pour the water.

"Hoo hoo hoo," I said. My chest suddenly itched a lot. I stopped to scratch it with both hands.

Then I stuck out my tongue at Ballantine and made a loud spitting noise.

His smile faded. He leaned forward in his big chair. He had a confused look on his face.

"Hoo hoo." I started to stand on my head.

But then I had an even better idea. I jumped onto the table. I kicked the top hat into the air. "Hoo hoo!" I cried. I scratched myself some more.

"Ha, ha!" Ballantine laughed. "He's a monkey. I get it! He's a monkey magician!"

Mr. and Mrs. Hocus started to laugh. And soon everyone in the back room at the store was laughing.

I made more spitting noises. I did a few cartwheels over the tabletop.

"Hoo hoo hoo."

Then I poured the pitcher of water over my head.

"Ha, ha, ha," Ballantine laughed some more. "Chimp magic. Look at him. He's very believable! Ha, ha!"

I wobbled off the stage. I felt kinda sick. That wasn't the trick I'd rehearsed.

Ballantine was laughing. Did that mean he liked it?

I wanted to climb a tree and hide on the highest limb and eat leaves.

But I saw him waving me over. He climbed down from his chair and led me to the side of the room.

My heart was pounding. I couldn't stop hopping up and down.

Ballantine rested his hand on my shoulder. "Chimp magic, huh?" he said softly. "Funny. Very original. It made me laugh, kid. But it's not what I'm looking for."

I pressed my lips together and made a loud spitting sound.

"Don't be disappointed," Ballantine said. "It was a nice try. But that monkey act just doesn't make it."

He patted my shoulder and gave me a gentle shove toward the door. "Come back in a few years—okay, Max?"

I slumped through the store. I gazed at the line of eager magicians. Two or three of them would be lucky. They would become students of Ballantine's.

But not me. I'd blown my big chance. I'd poured water on myself and spit in Ballantine's face.

How stupid was that?

And all because of my two ghost friends, Nicky and Tara.

Where were they? I wondered.

Had they tracked down that evil creep Smollet? They had to keep their promise. No way could I keep on going with this chimp brain inside me.

I pictured myself in school. Sitting in class. Pouring water over my head. Doing cartwheels. And spitting in Ms. McDonald's face.

"I need to get my brain back to normal!" I shouted.

Several magicians turned and gaped at me.

"Sorry," I said. "That's part of my act. Brain magic. Ha, ha. Hoo hoo."

I hurried across the street to my mom's car.

Now it was time for Traci's cousin's birthday party.

My big chance to be at a party with the coolest girl in school.

Could I keep my monkey brain under control?

26

TRACI'S COUSIN STELLA GREETED me at her door. She was a tiny girl with curly brown hair and pointy ears that poked out of her hair and stood straight up like mouse ears.

I knew she was a sixth grader like me. But she looked about four years old. And she was wearing a frilly, lacy party dress that made her look like some kind of doll that should be kept on a shelf.

"Hoo hoo. Happy birthday," I said. I handed her the present Mom had wrapped for me.

"Thanks," Stella said. "What is it?"

"I don't know," I said. "Something my mom picked out."

She tossed it into the house. "Do you have your flashlight?" she asked. "You can't come in unless you have it. It's a flashlight party."

I held up my flashlight. "Hoo hoo," I said. I hopped up and down and scratched Stella under the chin.

"That's not funny," she said. "Traci said you

were kind of odd." She pushed open the screen door. "I guess you can come in."

"Thanks," I said. "Hoo hoo. Traci said you were really awesome."

That was a total lie, but I was trying to be nice. I mean, it was her birthday and everything.

"Traci thinks I'm a wimp," Stella said. But a smile spread over her tiny face. "We're going to play Spin the Flashlight later. I'll show her who's a wimp!"

Spin the Flashlight?

This really *was* a flashlight party! My first!

Stella led me into the living room. It was decorated with pink and yellow balloons everywhere. And it was crowded with kids.

"Traci is already here," Stella said. She pointed. I saw Traci, her back to me.

"Hoo hoo," I said.

Stella squinted. "Why do you keep saying that, Max?"

I shrugged. "Just a bad habit," I said.

I started across the room. Kids were shining their flashlights into each other's eyes and laughing. Two boys were using their flashlights to poke each other in the stomach.

I knew they had to be sixth graders. But they all looked totally babyish.

"Hi, Traci," I said.

She turned around—and *smiled* at me!

I nearly fainted. Traci Wayne *smiled* at me!

"Max," she said, "compared to the drippy nerds in this room, you're almost okay."

Wow! A compliment!

"Hoo hoo," I said. I pulled up my shirt and scratched my belly with both hands.

Traci groaned. "I take back what I just said," she said.

Stella hurried over. "Max, why did you do that?"

"I'm a party animal," I said.

"It's time for our flashlight games," Stella said. She turned and shouted for everyone to pay attention. "Flashlight games, everyone! This is going to be way cool!"

"Hoo hoo," I said.

Traci leaned close and whispered in my ear. "Max, I'm warning you. Don't embarrass me."

"No problem," I said. I stuck out my tongue and spit all over her.

"Uck!" Traci cried, wiping my spit off her chin. "How funny are you? Not!" She hurried to the other side of the room.

I clenched my hands into fists. I knew I had to hold myself in. I had to be totally on guard at all times. No *way* did I want Traci to know about my little monkey problem.

I hung back and stayed quiet when the games began. But to my shock, the games went on for *hours.* You have no idea how many flashlight games there are!

Stella and most of the other kids seemed to be having a great time. Traci stayed against the wall, making calls on her cell phone to all her cool friends. I hung in another corner, trying not to act like a chimp and give myself away.

Finally, I couldn't help it. I opened my flashlight, pulled out a battery, and started sucking on it, making loud, disgusting sucking noises.

Do you have to ask why? Because I was part chimpanzee!

Stella stopped the game. Her mouth dropped open. "Max? What are you doing?" She started shouting for her mom.

Her mom came running into the room. She looked just like Stella, only maybe a few inches taller. She pulled the battery from my mouth. "Young man, are you trying to be funny?" she asked. "Do you know how dangerous this is?"

I saw Traci staring at me. She was blushing bright red.

I had totally embarrassed her.

Something inside me snapped. I wanted to be nice, well-mannered, quiet Max Doyle.

But I had a monkey problem. And there was nothing I could do about it.

The monkey took over. I wobbled to the food

table. I grabbed up a big hunk of potato salad and flung it at Stella's mom.

It hit her on the forehead with a wet smack and dripped down her face.

I heaved another pile of potato salad and hit the wall above the fireplace.

"Max! Stop it! Are you *crazy*? Stop it!"

That was Traci screaming at me.

Could I stop it? No way.

I climbed up on the food table. Raised a big bowl of pretzels above my head—and heaved it at a group of shocked kids across the room. Kids screamed as pretzels flew everywhere.

Then I dug both hands into the chocolate icing of the birthday cake, rubbed some of it in my hair, and flung a big hunk at Stella.

It hit her in the chin and dripped down her neck.

I was chattering like a chimp. I couldn't stop myself. I reached for two more handfuls of cake and saw Stella and her mom and Traci storm toward me.

Stella and her mom grabbed my arms and jerked me down to the floor. I struggled to climb back onto the table. But they held me tightly.

"Traci, take your friend home," Stella's mom commanded angrily. "He is acting like a wild animal. Take him home at once."

Traci's face was bright red. She was shaking

with anger and embarrassment. "I'm so sorry," she whispered, lowering her head. "I'm really so sorry."

She grabbed me and pulled me to the front door. "Max, what is your *problem*?" she asked through gritted teeth.

"Hoo hoo," I said.

I still had hunks of chocolate cake in my hands. I rubbed them in Traci's hair. Then I started grooming her with both hands.

Would she ever speak to me again?

Three guesses.

27

"**HOW WAS THE BIRTHDAY** party?" Mom asked.

"Great," I said.

"Did you make a lot of new friends?"

"Oh, sure," I said.

I hurried up to my room before I could start chimping it up again. "Nicky? Tara? Are you here?" I called, searching for them. "Where are you? Did you find Dr. Smollet?"

Silence. No sign of them.

I let out a long sigh. My life was ruined. Ruined forever.

I hopped onto my bed and began jumping up and down, making chattering noises.

Wait. Suddenly, I had a hunch. I just *knew* where I'd find Nicky and Tara.

Back at Dr. Smollet's lab. Don't ask me why. I had the strongest feeling that they were back there.

I had to go. I had to see if my hunch was right.

Mom was busy in the kitchen. I sneaked past her and let myself out the front door. The moon was already high in the sky. The night breeze felt cold against my face.

Wobbling like a chimp, I hurried to the bus stop.

I leaped onto a low tree limb and ate some leaves as I waited for the bus. It didn't come for nearly half an hour. Finally, I climbed inside and walked to the back.

"Hoo hoo." I wanted to swing on the poles, but I forced myself to stay in my seat.

The bus bumped along Miller Street, then turned when it got to town. There were two other kids on the bus, but they didn't go to my school.

I got off half a block from the lab. Seeing it again, my heart began to thump. My legs felt as if they weighed a thousand pounds as I pulled open the gate, walked past the barbed wire fence, and stepped up to the front door.

This is crazy, I thought. Why would Dr. Smollet come back here?

How can I even get in?

My hand shook. I tried the front door. Was it locked? No. I pulled it open easily.

As soon as I stepped inside, I heard the cries and howls of the lab animals hidden somewhere beyond the white walls. I wanted to find them and set them all free.

But I knew that getting my brain back to normal was more important right now.

I strode quickly down the twisting white halls. I was surprised that I remembered the way.

The door to the lab stood open. I took a deep breath and stepped inside.

"Oh!" I let out a cry when I saw Dr. Smollet and Mr. Harvey in the middle of the room.

A smile spread slowly over Dr. Smollet's face. "Come in, Max," he said. "Mr. Harvey and I have been waiting for you."

28

I **FROZE IN THE** doorway. My whole body locked in fear.

Before I could move, Dr. Smollet rushed across the room and grabbed me by the shoulders. He was surprisingly strong. He half-dragged, half-carried me to the tall stool beside all the computers.

And I realized that Mr. Harvey was already hooked up. The chimp had headphones on. He was sitting quietly, watching the whole thing.

Dr. Smollet took a cable and wrapped it tightly around my chest and arms. He quickly tied me to the tall stool beside the chimp.

"Wh-what are you going to do?" I finally managed to say.

He ran a hand through his white beard. His cold smile grew wider. "I'm going to finish the job," he said. "I only switched *half* your brains before. Now I'm going to complete the transfer. You will be a total chimp."

He reached for a set of headphones.

"But—why?" I choked out.

118

"Setting my trap," Dr. Smollet said. "Nicky and Tara's parents ruined my life. Now I'm going to trap the whole family and pay them back."

"What are you talking about?" I shouted.

"I didn't work for the Rolands. I worked for Phears. I've waited a long time to pay them back for what they did to us ghosts."

"By making me a chimp?" I said.

He nodded. "Nicky and Tara will do anything to save you—won't they? Even stay here with me in my lab? I'm going to make your two ghost friends a deal. I'll return your brain to normal—*if* they agree to stay here. You see, I'm going to use Nicky and Tara as bait to reel in their parents."

"Your plan will never work," I said. "Give me a chance to talk with Nicky and Tara. Maybe—"

He knew I was stalling for time. His blue eyes grew cold. He tightened the cables around me, making sure I couldn't escape. Then he moved to a computer keyboard and started typing.

I squirmed and struggled to pull myself free. I shook my head back and forth, trying to toss off the headphones.

The chimp chattered and hopped up and down on the stool next to me. I heard a low electronic hum.

I shut my eyes and clamped my teeth together.

Oh no. Oh no. This can't be happening, I thought.

He's going to suck out the last part of my brain. And leave me with a chimp brain. Max the Chimp. Max the Chimpbrain—forever.

The hum grew louder.

What could I do? I had to escape—but *how*?

The hum made my head vibrate. It grew louder till it drowned out all sound—even my *thoughts*!

And then I felt a soft puff of air inside my head. Like a puff of smoke, floating over my mind, blanking it out . . . blanking it all out.

I opened my eyes. I blinked several times, struggling to focus.

Dr. Smollet stood tensely at the keyboard, rubbing his beard, watching me.

I picked up my head. I scratched my chest.

"Hoo hoo hoo," I said.

29

I FELT LIKE HOPPING up and down. Then I thought how nice it would be to climb a tree and pick some tasty leaves.

But I couldn't move. I was tied to the stool.

"Hoo hoo."

"It worked," I heard Dr. Smollet say. "I am a genius. I have transferred a chimp's brain into a living boy."

"Hoo?"

I didn't understand. What was he talking about? Did he plan to set me free?

Where did he keep the bananas? Where were the trees for me to climb?

"Chee chee chee!" I called, trying to get his attention.

But something strange was happening to Dr. Smollet. He suddenly began acting totally weird.

His arms flew up. He spun around.

"Let me go!" he screamed. "Get off me! Nicky! Tara! Let me go!"

Who was he screaming at? I didn't see anyone else in the room except for the other chimp.

Dr. Smollet started staggering backward. He was thrashing his arms and shouting. It looked like someone was pushing him to the tall stools, except I couldn't see anyone there.

The next thing I knew, the other chimp was set free. I expected him to run away, but he didn't. He climbed down from the stool and stood scratching his head.

Squirming and kicking, Dr. Smollet plopped down on the stool next to me. "You can't do this to me!" he screamed. "Let me go! What are you doing? You two don't know how to switch brains!"

His angry words rang in my ears. What did they mean?

I watched the headphones fly up all by themselves. Then they slid down over Dr. Smollet's head.

I suddenly felt frightened. What was happening here?

Was something bad going to happen to me?

I tried to figure it all out, but thinking so hard made my head hurt. I wanted to climb to the highest tree branch I could find. But I wasn't even in my own body. I was in a *boy's* body! Trapped here. Trapped!

I heard a loud hum in the headphones. My head started to buzz. The buzz grew louder.

The last thing I saw was the terrified look on Dr. Smollet's face.

I felt a shock. I shut my eyes.

I felt a gentle puff of wind inside my head.

When I opened my eyes, everything had changed.

30

I SAW NICKY AND Tara standing by the computer keyboard. "You can't do this!" I screamed. "You can't do this to a great scientist!"

My voice came out high and shrill. I realized I was inside Max's body.

The two evil little Roland ghosts had made a successful switch. My brain was inside Max. And inside my body . . .

"Hoo hoo hoo!"

The chimp! Mr. Harvey's brain was now inside *my* body. The chimp was scratching *my* beard, slapping the front of *my* white lab coat.

I knew I'd never get over this insult. Putting the brain of a chimp inside the head of one of the world's most brilliant scientists!

I'll wait for my chance, I thought. I'll make those two ghosts pay for what they've done!

But what can I do? I'm just a boy. A brilliant scientist trapped in a boy's body!

Oh no. I gasped as I saw what those two ghost kids were doing.

They pulled my body—Dr. Smollet's body—off the other stool. They put the chimp on the stool and hooked him up with the headphones.

I knew what they planned to do.

The chimp had Max's brain inside him. And I—Dr. Smollet—was inside Max's body.

So I knew what they planned to do. And I knew I was helpless to stop them.

The loud hum in my ears again. A strong jolt of electricity. A pounding roar.

And then a gentle puff of air.

I opened my eyes. I glanced around.

Nicky and Tara ran up to me. They pulled the headphones off and tossed them to the floor. They helped me off the stool, onto the floor.

"Max? Max? Are you back to normal?" Tara cried.

"Did it work?" Nicky demanded, tugging my arm eagerly. "Did our brain transfer work, Max? Are you Max again? The right brain in the right body?"

"Hoo hoo hoo," I said.

31

I LAUGHED. "I'M ONLY kidding!" I cried. "I'm back. I have my brain back again! I'm so happy, I wish I could *kiss* it!"

I hugged them both. "Good work, guys! You saved me! This time, you *really* saved me!"

"Let's get out of here," Tara said. "This place gives me the creeps."

I turned back. "But—what about them?"

I watched Dr. Smollet and Mr. Harvey. Their brains were switched. Dr. Smollet was pounding his chest, going, *"Chee chee chee!"* Mr. Harvey was pacing back and forth angrily, his hands clasped behind his back.

"We're safe now," Nicky said. "Smollet's brain is tucked nicely inside the chimp. He can't do any evil in there."

"But what if they switch brains again?" I asked.

"No way," Tara said. She took the chimp by the hand. "We're taking Mr. Harvey to the zoo.

They'll find him very interesting since he's so smart."

Nicky laughed. "The smartest chimp in history! Maybe he'll be famous."

"The zoo will never let him go," Tara said. "Dr. Smollet will *never* get his brain back."

"Hoo hoo!" Dr. Smollet called.

We ran down the long hall, dragging the chimp with us. Out on the street, the night air felt fresh and cold.

I hugged Nicky and Tara again. Yes, my performance for Ballantine was ruined. But I was a lucky dude. Lucky to have such amazing friends.

I watched Nicky and Tara head off with Mr. Harvey, the brilliant chimpanzee. I hoped he enjoyed his new home.

Then I took the Miller Street bus back to my house.

Mom was in the kitchen, grinding stuff in the food processor. "Max? Where have you been?" She had to shout over the deafening roar of the machine.

"I was kidnapped by a crazed ghost scientist. I traded brains with a chimpanzee," I told her. "Then we traded back."

"That's nice," she shouted. "Now go upstairs and do your homework."

"No problem," I said.

• • •

The next Saturday, Mom surprised me with two tickets. Two tickets to see Ballantine the Nearly Amazing in an all-star performance at the City Center!

Can you imagine how excited I felt? I'd never seen the great magician do his act live. And our seats were in the *second* row!

Before the curtain, I could barely sit still. Finally, the lights went dim. The huge auditorium grew silent.

A white spotlight moved across the deep purple curtain. And a voice boomed over the loudspeaker: "Ladies and gentlemen, we are proud to present the world-famous magician Ballantine the Nearly Amazing. Tonight he will be performing the new comedy-magic act he calls Monkey Magic. Let's hear it for Ballantine!"

The crowd cheered. The purple curtain rose slowly. I saw a carnival set. A table loaded with magic equipment.

And out came Ballantine in his glittery cape and turban, wobbling like a chimp. He turned to the audience and called out, "Hoo hoo hoo!"

The audience roared. They thought it was a riot.

Ballantine, acting like a monkey! He climbed onto the table and peeled a banana. He made the banana disappear back into the peel.

"Hoo hoo!" he called.

The audience roared and cheered.

I sat back in my seat, my mouth hanging open.

Mom turned to me. "Max? You're not enjoying it?" she whispered. "What's wrong?"

"He . . . he stole my act!" I cried.

TO BE CONTINUED

ABOUT THE AUTHOR

Robert Lawrence Stine's scary stories have made him one of the bestselling children's authors in history. "Kids like to be scared!" he says, and he has proved it by selling more than 300 million books. R.L. teamed up with Parachute Press to create Fear Street, the first and number one bestselling young adult horror series. He then went on to launch Goosebumps, the creepy bestselling series that gave kids chills all over the world and made him the number one children's author of all time (*The Guinness Book of Records*).

R.L. Stine lives in Manhattan with his wife, Jane, their son, Matthew, and their dog, Nadine. He says he has never seen a ghost—but he's still looking!

Be sure to check out the next book
in the Mostly Ghostly series,

Don't Close Your Eyes!

IN A TERRIFYING EPISODE, an evil sleep ghost named
Inkweed has inhabited Max. The ghost has come to
put Nicky and Tara to sleep forever.

But Inkweed is powerless until Max goes to
sleep. He stays dormant inside Max, waiting for
the moment when Max closes his eyes so that he
can bring his crushing evil powers to life.

Nicky and Tara frantically work to keep Max
awake—until they can come up with a scheme to
rid him of Inkweed. Days go by, and poor sleep-
deprived Max gets crazier and crazier. He's desperate for sleep. But if he closes his eyes, it will
mean the end of all three of them.

Can Nicky and Tara find a way to banish
Inkweed before Max closes his eyes?

ALL THREE OF US stared down at the open book on the floor, frozen in shock.

The words written about the evil ghost Inkweed slid quickly to the middle and formed a black puddle of ink. The puddle spread silently over the book, growing wider and deeper.

"This is *crazy*!" I cried.

And then we gasped as the ink puddle began to rise off the book. It lifted itself up as if it was alive! A living ink creature.

"Inkweed is alive!" Tara screamed. Then she and Nicky flickered and faded. The shock was taking away their energy force.

But I could see the horror on their faces as the ink blob floated up into the air. It made a wet slapping sound as it settled against the bedroom wall. Then it began to shift and spread.

"Stop it! We have to *stop* it!" Tara screamed.

Nicky flickered in and out like a firefly. "H-how?" he stammered.

I jumped up from my desk chair and started to

back up, moving away from the shadowy ink blob as it spread over my wall.

It continued to spread, and then it pulled itself into a new shape. Slowly, slowly, it started to form a black, inky figure—the silhouette of a man!

"Is it . . . is it *Inkweed*?" Tara choked out.

Before anyone could answer, the inky shadow pulled off the wall—and floated over my head.

I ducked.

I tried to dodge it.

But it settled over me. Hot and wet. Like someone dropping a heavy wet bath towel over me.

I couldn't move. I couldn't see.

The dark shadow held me in place. It wrapped around me. My skin prickled under the hot wetness of it. Shiver after shiver rolled down my body.

I tried to cry out, but my voice was muffled under the thick, black shadow.

The shadow grew heavier. I bent over. Dropped to my knees under its weight.

I tried to scream. I tried to thrash my arms and duck my head to escape the terrifying blanket.

But I was frozen beneath it.

And then I felt it shift and start to settle. It was settling over me. No. Not settling.

Sinking.

Sinking into me!

Sinking into my skin. Into my *brain*!

My arms jerked. My head was flung back as if someone had slugged me.

I toppled over. My head hit the floor.

I felt as if I was swimming in blackness. Deep underwater in a freezing black pond. I felt the wet currents splashing inside me, one after the other.

And then I was back on my feet. Still squinting through a thick curtain of gray. Still shivering. Shaking my head, trying to shake the dark clouds away.

"Max!" Tara cried. Her shout sounded very far away. "Max! Are you okay?"

"Oh, wow." I heard Nicky's voice somewhere on the other side of the black curtain. "Max, you're covered in black ink. You're dripping!"

"Never mind that!" I shouted, surprised to hear my normal voice. "It's *inside* me! I can feel it!"

"Inkweed?" Nicky asked. "Is it Inkweed?"

The dark curtain lifted a little. I could see the two ghosts gaping at me in horror.

"I don't know what it is," I said. "But I can feel it inside my body! Inside my *head*!"

"Oh no. Oh no," Tara moaned, tugging her hat down over her ears.

"*Do* something!" I screamed. "Pick up the book! Hurry! You've got to help me. What does it say to do?"

Where Is
the Grand Canyon?

by Jim O'Connor

illustrated by Daniel Colón

Grosset & Dunlap
An Imprint of Penguin Group (USA) LLC

For Teddy, who asked me to visit the
Grand Canyon with him—JOC

For my parents, who taught
me to love the outdoors—DC

GROSSET & DUNLAP
Published by the Penguin Group
Penguin Group (USA) LLC, 375 Hudson Street, New York, New York 10014, USA

USA | Canada | UK | Ireland | Australia | New Zealand | India | South Africa | China

penguin.com
A Penguin Random House Company

Text copyright © 2015 by Jim O'Connor. Illustrations copyright © 2015 by Penguin Group (USA) LLC. All rights reserved. Published by Grosset & Dunlap, a division of Penguin Young Readers Group, 345 Hudson Street, New York, New York 10014. GROSSET & DUNLAP is a trademark of Penguin Group (USA) LLC. Printed in the USA.

Library of Congress Cataloging-in-Publication Data is available.

ISBN 978-0-448-48357-3   10 9 8 7 6 5 4 3 2 1

Contents

Where Is the Grand Canyon?

The Grand Canyon in Arizona is one of the United States' fifty-nine national parks. All are special wilderness areas that are protected by the US government. President Franklin Roosevelt said, "There is nothing so American as our national parks." Why? Because the parks belong to all the people of our country. They are not private property.

Back when the United States was a young country with limitless open space, not many people saw a need to set aside land for parks.

Even if there had been big parks, few people could have visited them. The majority of Americans worked six days a week. Not many had the time or money to travel more than a few miles from their home.

The first public park in the United States was the Boston Common, in Massachusetts, which was established in 1634. It was both a park and a common grazing area for cows.

In the 1830s, Americans began building cemeteries that were more than places to bury the dead. They had winding roads, ponds, landscaped hills, beautiful statues, and fancy mausoleums. (Mausoleums are like little houses with the dead buried inside them.)

People went to these beautiful cemeteries to have picnics and stroll around the grounds admiring the views. Cemeteries became popular as a kind of public park.

The idea of parks protected by the government began in the mid 1800s. The population was growing. More cities were sprouting all over the country, taking over large areas of land. A small

but important group of people realized that the United States had great natural treasures that needed to be preserved for all Americans forever.

For instance, Yosemite, an area in northern California, was known for its special trees. They were called giant sequoias. Some were over three thousand years old. They grew up to three hundred feet high with amazingly thick trunks. A group of Americans wanted to protect Yosemite's giant sequoia groves from logging and development. In 1864, President Abraham Lincoln made Yosemite a California state park.

The first area to be named a national park was Yellowstone in Wyoming. (Parts of the park are also in Montana and Idaho.)

Yellowstone is a special place because it is home to most of the world's geysers. A geyser is an underground spring of boiling-hot water that erupts through the surface of the earth. Yellowstone's most famous geyser is called Old

Faithful. In fact, it is the most famous geyser in the world. Every ninety-one minutes, Old Faithful erupts, spraying water 125 feet into the air. Yellowstone National Park was created in 1872 under a law signed by President Ulysses S. Grant.

The US Army

In the early days, Yellowstone and other national parks like Yosemite and Glacier in Montana were supervised by the United States Army. But army troops only spent the summer months in the parks. During the rest of the year, troops carried out their duties as soldiers. With only part-time help, it was very difficult to plan and complete long-term projects in the parks. So, in 1916, Congress created the National Park Service to supervise all the national parks.

The president who did the most for national parks was Theodore Roosevelt. He was in office from 1901 to 1909 and is often called the "conservation president." He wanted to conserve—keep and protect—the beauty of nature in the United States.

President Roosevelt grew up in New York City, but he was a real outdoorsman. As a young man, he became a cattle rancher out west in North Dakota. All his life he loved to hunt and camp out under the stars. He wanted Americans and visitors from other countries to enjoy the beauty of the United States in its most unspoiled form.

More than a century ago Roosevelt saw how dangerous industry could be to natural resources such as water and forests. He said, "We have become great because of the lavish use of our resources. But the time has come to inquire seriously what will happen when our forests are gone, when the coal, the iron, the oil, and the gas are exhausted, when the soils have still further impoverished and washed into the streams, polluting the rivers, denuding the fields and obstructing navigation."

In 1903 he visited the Grand Canyon.

Here's his description: "In the Grand Canyon, Arizona has a natural wonder which is in kind absolutely unparalleled throughout the rest of the world." By that, he meant there was no place else like it. Roosevelt said, "You cannot improve on it.

The ages have been at work on it, and man can only mar it."

In the summer of 1913, Roosevelt returned to the Grand Canyon with his sons Archie and Quentin. During their vacation, they rode horses along the rim of the canyon and hunted cougars. Roosevelt wrote about his trip, calling the Grand Canyon "the most wonderful scenery in the world." He said, "Very wealthy men can have private game preserves of their own. But the average man . . . can enjoy wild nature, only if . . .

there are big parks or reserves provided for the use of all our people."

In 1919, Grand Canyon became a national park.

National Parks

Wrangell-St. Elias in Alaska is our largest national park. It covers over thirteen million acres. (That is bigger than the states of Maryland and Delaware combined.) American Samoa National Park is the smallest, with only 13,500 acres. Four thousand five hundred acres of that park are underwater coral reefs. In terms of size, Grand Canyon is the eleventh-largest national park. However, it is the second-most visited, with five million tourists coming

Glacier

Yellowstone

Yosemite

Grand Canyon

Wrangell-St. Elias

every year. Great Smoky Mountains National Park in Tennessee and North Carolina is the most popular, with nine million visitors a year.

Great Smoky Mountains

N

0   100   200
Miles

CHAPTER 1
Birth of a Canyon

Every year five million people from all over the world travel to northern Arizona to see the Grand Canyon. Driving north to the Grand Canyon from Phoenix, Sedona, or Flagstaff, the road gradually climbs to the top of what is called the Colorado Plateau. (A plateau is a large elevated flat area of land.)

There are plenty of signs for the Grand Canyon. All the hotels, restaurants, and stores for tourists announce that you are getting closer. The first sight of the canyon itself doesn't come until visitors arrive at the South Rim. Even then their view of the canyon is masked by trees and bushes. They must pull off the road at Mather Point Overlook, leave their cars, and walk a short

distance to the rim of the Grand Canyon. Then—
WOW! Suddenly they look down. People cannot
help but gasp in surprise at what they see.

What Is a Canyon?

A canyon is a deep, steep-sided gorge that is usually created by erosion. Sometimes earthquakes contribute to the formation of canyons. The deepest canyon in the world is Yarlung Tsangpo Grand Canyon in Tibet. At one point, it is sixteen thousand feet deep. That is more than three miles. The longest canyon in the world was discovered in 2013. It is hidden beneath a glacier in Greenland and goes for at least 460 miles. It has not even been named yet.

The Grand Canyon twists and turns for 270 miles. It is eighteen miles across at its widest point. This massive canyon was formed by the constant erosion of the Colorado River for the last six million years.

The river has cut through thousands of different layers of rock, so that now the canyon is over a mile deep. The "youngest" rock, near the top, is 250 million years old. The oldest—at the bottom—was formed two billion years ago.

As visitors gaze into the depths of the Grand Canyon, the shifting rays of the sun light up rock formations, smaller side canyons, and amazing colored layers of rock. Some are bright orange, some are golden brown, some are pink and white. Late in the day when the sun begins to set, the landscape turns violet, then darkens to purple before it disappears into the darkness.

At first glance, the Grand Canyon seems empty, but it is teeming with wildlife and countless varieties of plants. The scale is so huge that a boulder larger than a three-story building looks like a small rock to visitors at the rim. Even the mighty Colorado River seems tiny when seen from a mile above.

Seven Natural Wonders of the World

The Grand Canyon is listed as one of the Seven Natural Wonders of the World. There are many lists of World Wonders. They usually include the Great Wall of China, the Great Pyramids in Egypt, and whichever building is the tallest skyscraper at the time the list is made. All have one thing in common—they are man-made.

The seven greatest natural wonders have been created over millions of years as the earth formed and changed. Besides the Grand Canyon, here are the six others most people agree on:

The Great Barrier Reef in Australia is the largest coral reef in the world. Covering approximately 133,000 square miles, it is so large it can be seen from outer space.

Mount Everest is the highest mountain on earth.

Its summit is 29,029 feet high. Everest straddles the border of Tibet and Nepal.

Victoria Falls in Africa is the largest waterfall in the world. It is on the border of Zambia and Zimbabwe.

The auroras are natural light shows that occur high in the northern and southern skies. They usually look like green or purple curtains that pulse and change shape continuously.

Brazil's Great Harbor of Rio de Janeiro is the largest harbor in the world. It covers about four hundred square miles.

Paricutín in Mexico is a cinder cone volcano that suddenly began erupting in 1943 and continued until 1952. It is 1,391 feet tall and covers an area of about twenty square miles.

CHAPTER 2
Native People

Native Americans have lived in and around the canyon for at least the last ten thousand years.

The first humans to see the Grand Canyon were bands of hunters who roamed the American Southwest. When they first stood at the rim of the canyon, they would have looked at the same incredibly colorful rock formations seen today.

In fact, except for a few recent buildings scattered along the South Rim of the Grand Canyon, almost everything these ancient people saw looks the same now. Ten thousand years is just a blink of the eye in the formation of a canyon that is at least six million years old.

These first visitors were nomads who traveled and hunted throughout the Southwest. They did not build permanent homes or villages. Some of the animals they hunted still live in the Grand Canyon—deer, antelope, bighorn sheep, and rabbits.

The only trace these ancient people left behind are the spearheads they used for hunting bighorn sheep and deer. Archeologists call these people Paleo-Indians. Paleo means "ancient."

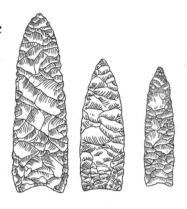

Between two thousand and four thousand years ago, other groups of nomadic hunters came to the canyon. They are called the Desert Culture, and they made figures of animals from willow twigs they split and bent. These figures were left in hundreds of limestone caves that are cut into the canyon's walls. They were probably gifts to their gods.

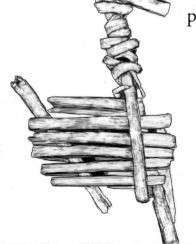

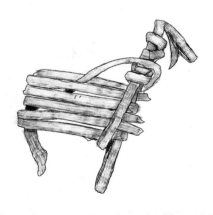

Some of these original split-twig figures are on display at the park's Tusayan Museum. Tusayan is the ruin of an eight-hundred-year-old village that was built by the Pueblo Indians. It is located about twenty-five miles east of Grand Canyon Village, near the Desert View Watchtower.

The next native people to live in the canyon were the Anasazi. They arrived on the Colorado Plateau roughly 1,500 years ago. Their name comes from the Navajo word that means "Ancient Ones" or "Ancient Enemy." The Anasazi were hunters and farmers. They hunted deer, antelope, and sheep. In the summer they planted corn, beans, and squash. They also gathered and ate piñon nuts, pods from yucca trees, and cactus fruit.

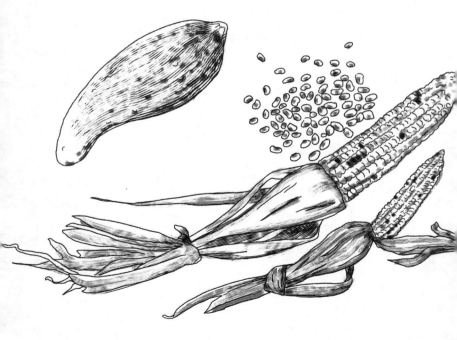

The Anasazi wove beautiful baskets and made sandals, clay bowls, and other items. In the winter they used deerskin and rabbit fur to make capes and blankets.

In the late twelfth century, a dry spell forced the Anasazi to abandon the Grand Canyon and move south and east to the Hopi Mesas and Rio Grande Valley.

Not long after the Anasazi left the Grand Canyon, other Native American tribes began to arrive. First came the Hopi. They have lived around the Grand Canyon for over a thousand years. One of their villages, Oraibi, is probably the oldest community in the United States—it's over eight hundred years old! Today Hopi Indians live on a small reservation surrounded by a much larger reservation belonging to Navajo Indians.

Navajo and Hopi Indians have lived near each other for centuries. There have been many disagreements between the two tribes. The Navajo became sheepherders starting in the late 1400s. That's when Spanish explorers first brought sheep to the Southwest. The Hopi, however, have always been farmers, raising crops such as corn and beans. They have resented sheep grazing because it ruins the land for farming.

Another tribe of hunters—the Southern Paiute—lived on the Kaibab plateau north of the canyon. (Kaibab means "mountain turned upside down" in the Paiute language.) They first came to the Grand Canyon around 1300 AD.

The Havasupai tribe's reservation land cuts right through the canyon. In fact, the Havasupai are the only tribe remaining in the canyon today. Their 188,077-acre reservation borders the western edge of Grand Canyon National Park. Their name means "people of the blue-green water." It refers to the blue Havasu Creek and its spectacular waterfalls. This is a popular but remote area. It can only be reached by hiking, by mule, or by helicopter. The Havasupai own and operate a hotel and campground near the creek and waterfalls.

The Zuni, who live in northern New Mexico today, also lived in the Grand Canyon. They have a unique language that is unlike any other Native American dialect.

Another canyon-area tribe is the Hualapai. Hualapai means "people of the tall pines." They have never lived in the canyon but hunt and farm west of the park. In 2007, they built Grand

Canyon Skywalk. It is a glass-bottom observation platform. It allows visitors to look straight down to the canyon floor. Tourists are amazed by the thrilling view.

However, for the Native Americans who have lived in the region for so long, the canyon is important for much more than its scenery. The Grand Canyon is a place filled with great spiritual meaning. The Zuni, for example, regard certain waterfalls in the canyon as sacred places.

Most Native American tribes believe in the Flood Myth—a story that tells of a new beginning for the world after a great flood. The Hopi believe that the flood took place at the Grand Canyon. Hopi men still make pilgrimages to the Grand Canyon. They come to collect salt from a mine near the Colorado River. The salt is used in their tribal rituals.

For all these native people, the Grand Canyon is first and foremost a sacred site, one that must be treated with respect and protected for future generations.

CHAPTER 3
Cities of Gold

In 1540, a group from Spain led by Francisco Vásquez de Coronado was exploring the southwest of North America. They were searching for the Seven Cities of Cíbola, which according to legend were filled with treasures.

Twenty years earlier, another explorer, Hernando Cortés, had conquered the Aztec people of Mexico. Cortés had sent incredible treasures home to Spain. Coronado believed that the seven cities with all their riches lay farther north in what is now Arizona. He wanted to send treasure back to Spain and be famous like Cortés.

Coronado's group found nothing more than a

small Native American village where the cities of gold were supposed to be. There was no treasure. Coronado, however, was not ready to give up. He sent out a search party to look farther west for the cities of Cíbola. These men had no success, either. But they did tell Coronado that there was a large and powerful river that might lead to the seven cities.

So Coronado sent out yet another search party. It was led by García López de Cárdenas. This group didn't find the cities of Cíbola, either.

What they did "discover," however, was the Grand Canyon. They were the first Europeans to lay eyes on it. When they looked down from the canyon's South Rim, the Spaniards thought that the river flowing far below was only six feet wide! How could this be the mighty river that they'd been sent to find? (In reality the Colorado averages three hundred feet across.)

Still, Cárdenas ordered some of the men to walk down into the canyon and look around. It was tough going. There was no trail down the steep canyon walls. As they got deeper into the canyon, the men realized the rocks that looked so small from up on the rim were, in fact, giant boulders. Some were almost two hundred feet high. (That's as tall as a twenty-story building.)

Finally the men gave up trying to reach the bottom of the canyon and climbed back up. They told Cárdenas what they had seen, and he decided to return to Coronado. That was the end of the search for the cities of gold. However, the Spanish continued to rule an area that is now Arizona, New Mexico, Texas, and southern California for another three hundred years.

The arrival of Spanish explorers had a major impact on native peoples in the area of the Grand Canyon. The Spanish brought horses, sheep, and cattle to the Southwest. This forever changed how native tribes lived and where they traveled.

It wasn't until 1776 that a Spanish priest named the canyon's river Colorado, which is Spanish for "colored red." When he saw the river for the first time, it was during the spring floods. Red silt had washed down from the desert, making the water look red.

The United States acquired the land that includes the Grand Canyon in 1803. It was part of what is called the Louisiana Purchase. President Thomas Jefferson bought a huge area of land for less than three cents an acre. Settlers, however, were more interested in the northern regions of the Louisiana Purchase. Animals like beaver and

Thomas Jefferson

buffalo lived there. They were valuable for their fur.

Not until 1857 did the United States government send a group to explore the lower Colorado River. It was led by Lieutenant Joseph Christmas Ives. Ives ran his steamship, *Explorer,* aground many times until he finally wrecked it. He was not at all impressed by what he saw of the Grand Canyon. In a report sent to Washington, DC, Ives wrote, "The region . . . is, of course, altogether valueless."

Joseph Ives

CHAPTER 4
A One-Armed Adventurer

The first group to explore the Grand Canyon from end to end was led by John Wesley Powell in 1869. Powell had been a soldier in the Civil War. He had lost his right arm in battle. Powell's men always referred to him as "the Major."

John Wesley Powell

Powell was a geologist—he was interested in the study of rocks and the earth's layers. He was convinced that the Grand Canyon offered a great opportunity to study millions of years of the earth's history. He kept a detailed journal of everything he saw.

He took a group of nine men exploring in four wooden boats. They started on May 26, 1869, on Utah's Green River. They had enough supplies for ten months. Within the first month one boat was wrecked and half of the supplies were lost, so they were always short on food. One of the men quit and went home. Powell and the others continued in the remaining three boats.

Early in the trip Powell narrowly avoided a fatal fall. On July 8, Powell and another man named George Bradley decided to measure the height of the cliffs above the river. Even with just one arm, Powell had climbed cliffs many times. So had Bradley. They took no ropes or safety gear with them.

Powell and Bradley made steady progress until they were about six hundred feet above the river. Suddenly they began to have more difficulty finding a route to the top. Powell was leading. He edged out onto a narrow ledge and saw a place to hold above his head. With his one arm, Powell stretched and grabbed the rock. However, he quickly realized that he was trapped. If he let go of the rock, there was nothing else for him to hold on to.

There was no way to go, up or down.

Powell's muscles began to cramp. Bradley had no time to go for help. He had to act quickly to save Powell.

Luckily Bradley found a way to reach a ledge above Powell. He leaned over. Right away he realized that Powell was too far below him. He couldn't reach down to catch Powell's wrist.

Bradley had a sudden, desperate plan. He had climbed the cliff just wearing a shirt, pants, and long underwear. He stripped off his clothes and

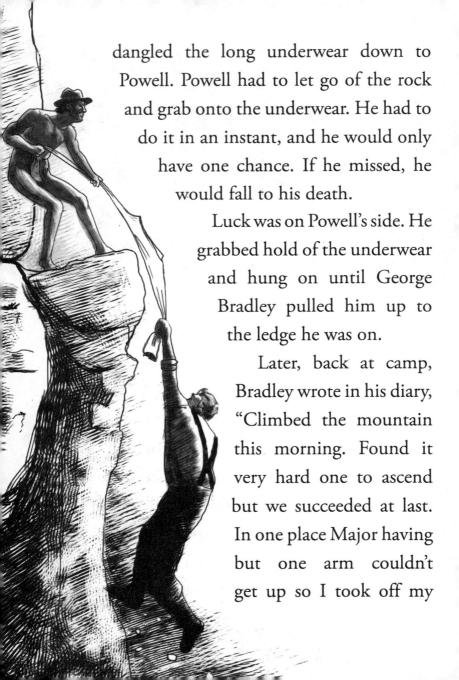

dangled the long underwear down to Powell. Powell had to let go of the rock and grab onto the underwear. He had to do it in an instant, and he would only have one chance. If he missed, he would fall to his death.

Luck was on Powell's side. He grabbed hold of the underwear and hung on until George Bradley pulled him up to the ledge he was on.

Later, back at camp, Bradley wrote in his diary, "Climbed the mountain this morning. Found it very hard one to ascend but we succeeded at last. In one place Major having but one arm couldn't get up so I took off my drawers and they made an excellent substitute for rope and with that assistance he got up safe."

Powell and his men did not reach the Colorado River until July 17. One day Powell and his men discovered a small stream flowing into the Colorado. Powell named it Bright Angel Creek because the water was clear and bright compared to the muddy brown Colorado. Today the main route from Grand Canyon Village down to the river is called Bright Angel Trail, as it ends right at this spot.

Powell and his men were traveling through uncharted waters. They had no idea where they were going or what lay ahead. It was very dangerous. There were hundreds of wild rapids that could easily turn their boats into toothpicks and drown all the men. No one in Powell's group had any experience running rapids.

Their boats were all wrong for the trip. They should have had light, flat-bottomed boats that would ride high in the water and glide over hidden rocks. Their boats, however, were heavy rowboats, called dories. Dories sat deep in the water and were hard to steer. Worst of all, the men rowed facing upstream. That meant they could not see where to steer when they hit rapids.

Whenever possible they portaged around dangerous rapids. "Portaging" means they carried the boats along the side of the canyon.

After three months, they came to the most dangerous-looking set of rapids yet. The canyon walls were sheer stone rising hundreds of feet. There was no way to portage.

Right then and there, three men decided to leave the expedition. Powell tried to persuade them to stay, but they would not change their minds. So Powell said good-bye and wished them well. The men set off to hike out of the canyon and were never seen again.

As luck would have it, Powell and the rest of his men had no difficulty getting through the rapids that day. (Powell named the spot Separation Rapids in honor of the men who left him there.) The following day, August 29, 1869, the Powell Expedition reached the very western end of the Grand Canyon.

Their journey was complete.

Death in the Grand Canyon

Like any wilderness area, the Grand Canyon can be dangerous if a person is not careful. The rough count is now around seven hundred deaths since tourists started coming to the Grand Canyon in the 1870s. Many times people get hurt because they do not use common sense. They stand too close to the edge of the canyon and fall. Or they don't take enough water on hikes. Animal attacks are very rare, and no one has ever died from a rattlesnake bite there.

The worst disaster at the park took place in 1956. Two airplanes collided over the canyon, killing all 128 passengers and crew.

The 1869 trip was not the only one Powell made to the area. He returned to the canyon several times. In 1871, he brought a photographer with him, who took some of the very first pictures of the Grand Canyon.

Powell kept a detailed journal of each trip and published the report. The book was called *Exploration of the Colorado River of the West and Its Tributaries*. (A tributary is a smaller river that flows into a bigger one.)

Powell became famous and gave many lectures about his adventures. His book brought lots of attention to the Grand Canyon. Before long, other Americans began exploring the canyon.

Miners came searching for copper, gold, or lead. Prospecting in the Grand Canyon was very difficult. Some of the miners gave up the hunt for metal and found a different way to make money. They started renting tents to tourists from back east. Before long the tent village was replaced by hotels.

In 1901, the Santa Fe Railroad ran a spur line to Grand Canyon Village. Now tourists could travel to the Grand Canyon easily instead of taking a bumpy eleven-hour stagecoach ride from Flagstaff, Arizona. The railroad company also built a fancy hotel. It was called the El Tovar and is still in business. By 1919, more than forty thousand tourists had visited the Grand Canyon in one year.

CHAPTER 5
A Layer Cake of Rock

The Grand Canyon is located in a 130,000-square-mile region called the Colorado Plateau. The plateau covers northern Arizona, southern Utah, the southwest corner of Colorado, and part of northwest New Mexico. (It also contains ten national parks, including Grand Canyon.)

Most of the plateau consists of thousands of layers of sedimentary rock formed when ancient oceans covered the area. When the oceans disappeared, the plateau remained.

So how was the Grand Canyon made? The simple answer is erosion from the river. For millions of years the Colorado River cut its way through many layers of different rock. Little by little, the river sliced into the land—a slice that is nearly three hundred miles long and over a mile deep.

Erosion from the Colorado River, however, is not the only reason the canyon exists. The desert terrain of the Southwest does not encourage plant growth. Without plants and their root systems to hold soil, more erosion occurs.

Although the Southwest has an arid—or dry— climate, it does rain and snow at the canyon at times. And when it does, the storms are violent. Rainfall is hard, and this speeds erosion, too. The yearly winter rains run down the canyon walls and wash sand, pebbles, rocks, and boulders into the gorge.

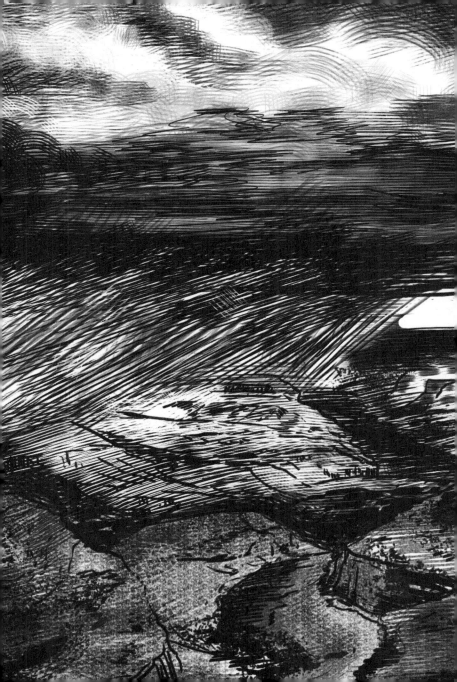

Winter rains also collect in cracks in the canyon walls and freeze. Water expands when it freezes, making the cracks wider. Finally, the rock breaks off from the canyon wall and crashes to the bottom.

Rainwater erosion also washes away softer layers of rock that have supported harder rock. The harder rock loosens and eventually falls down into the canyon.

Wind has also played a part in shaping the canyon. Many of the mesas and buttes that are so amazing to see were formed by millions of years of wind brushing tiny bits of rock away one bit at a time.

Mesas and Buttes

A mesa is a flat-topped hill or mountain with very steep sides. It is always wider than it is tall. The word "mesa" means "table" in Spanish.

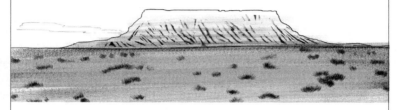

Buttes are smaller than mesas. They are taller than they are wide. Both mesas and buttes are found throughout the southwestern United States.

Because of all the erosion, visitors to the Grand Canyon today can see at least eleven different layers of rock. These layers lie one right on top of another, like a layer cake. The oldest rocks are the bottom layer, and the youngest, the top.

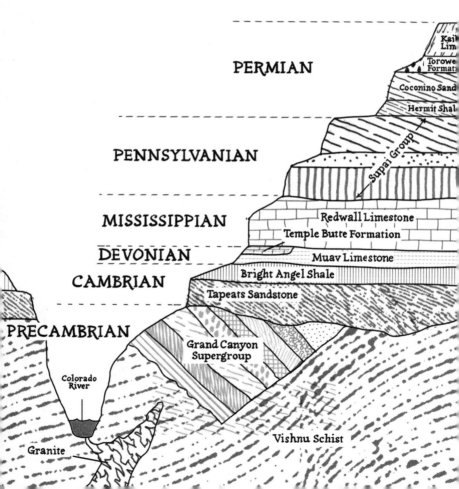

PERMIAN

PENNSYLVANIAN

MISSISSIPPIAN

DEVONIAN

CAMBRIAN

PRECAMBRIAN

Kai
Lim
Torowe
Format
Coconino Sand
Hermit Shal
Supai Group
Redwall Limestone
Temple Butte Formation
Muav Limestone
Bright Angel Shale
Tapeats Sandstone
Grand Canyon
Supergroup
Colorado
River
Vishnu Schist
Granite

The oldest rock is called the Vishnu Schist. It is 1.7 billion years old and mostly black in color. The next oldest layer consists of pink sedimentary and igneous rock. It is between 800 million and 1.2 billion years old.

On top of the pink rock is a layer called the Tapeats Sandstone. It is packed with fossilized sponges and other sea creatures. These are proof that an ocean covered the area 545 million years ago.

On top of that layer is shale. It's blue gray in color and is 515 million years old. The shale is topped by limestone containing tiny bits of shells. Again this is evidence of another prehistoric ocean. The next layer, the Temple Butte Formation, which is a purplish limestone, also has many marine fossils.

At this point the canyon walls become much steeper. The next layer, which consists of more limestone, is eight hundred feet high and was formed 340 million years ago. Although it is mainly silver gray, iron oxide in the rocks has stained parts a deep red.

Topping this thick layer is a mix of sandstone, shale, and siltstone. In it are fossils of insects and ferns. Just above that is more shale, and then sandstone from dunes of a desert that covered the plateau 275 million years ago. It, in turn, is covered by the darker yellow-gray Toroweap Formation made of gypsum and shale and some sandstone. The very top layer of the plateau is cream-colored limestone.

In his journal, John Wesley Powell often wrote about the amazing rock formations and layers of rock that he and his group passed by. Most of his observations were precise and written in scientific language. But occasionally his writing becomes poetic. When he came upon beds of lava he wrote, "What a conflict of water and fire there must have been here! Just imagine a river of molten rock, running down into a river of melted snow. What a seething and boiling of the waters; what clouds of steam rolled into the heavens."

What's in a Name?

The Grand Canyon has thousands of rock masterpieces, and many of the most famous ones have names. Some are named after explorers, like Powell Point and Cardenas Butte.

Many are named after Native American tribes—Hopi Point, Pima Point, Yavapai Point, Coconino Plateau, Comanche Point, and Navajo Point.

There are also names from ancient Egypt, like Osiris Temple and Isis Temple. And a whole group take their names from the legends of King Arthur and the Knights of the Round Table—Lancelot Point, Guinevere Castle, Gawain Abyss, Galahad Point, King Arthur Castle, and Holy Grail Temple.

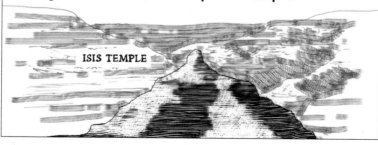

ISIS TEMPLE

CHAPTER 6
Wildlife in the Canyon

First-time visitors usually are blown away by the sight of the canyon itself. All the rock! They are unaware of the incredible number of animals and plants that make the Grand Canyon their home.

Riding the canyon's swirling air currents are bald eagles, ravens, red-tailed hawks, turkey vultures, and other birds of prey, which are also called "raptors." Every year in September and October, National Park Service rangers lead groups of bird-watchers to identify and count various types of raptors flying over the canyon.

In addition to the raptors, there are 350 different species of birds that fly over or live inside the canyon.

At the bottom of the canyon, there are seventeen kinds of freshwater fish that live in the Colorado River or its feeder streams. There are forty-seven reptile species, including geckos, lizards, Gila monsters, iguanas, and three kinds of rattlesnakes.

Mountain lion

Gila monster

There are all kinds of mammals, from small creatures such as chipmunks, squirrels, mice, weasels, porcupines, raccoons, and bats to big bears, elk, deer, sheep, mountain lions, and mule deer.

Depending on the time of year, visitors might glimpse elk near Grand Canyon Village. They are called Roosevelt elk and were brought to Grand Canyon Park after a native species of elk was killed off by hunters in the early 1900s.

Roosevelt elk

For thousands of years, people have hunted bighorn sheep, mountain lions, black bears, and mule deer in and around the Grand Canyon. The mountain lions also hunt the elk and deer. In fact, naturalists say that the average mountain lion kills one deer or elk per week at the canyon. This keeps the elk and deer population under control so they will have enough food to eat.

At night thousands of bats emerge from caves in the canyon's walls and consume tons of flying insects.

Only in the Canyon

The pink Grand Canyon rattlesnake is found nowhere else in the world. The snake can grow to over four feet long and has a unique pink color. That allows it to blend in with rocks of the same color in the lower canyon.

Besides the pink rattlesnake, there is also a species of squirrel—the Kaibab squirrel—that is found only in the canyon and only on its North Rim. Kaibabs are light gray in color with black bellies and snow-white tails. Long tasseled ears are its most unusual feature. Unlike most squirrels, Kaibabs don't store food for the winter. They eat the seeds of ponderosa pinecones as well as the bark of the tree.

The most dangerous animal in the Grand Canyon—at least, to tourists—is a small, furry, cute creature called the rock squirrel. Rock squirrels gather in busy areas because they use humans as vending machines.

Tourists try to lure the squirrels for pictures by holding out nuts, sandwiches, fruit, and other treats. Often tourists end up getting bitten. Besides being painful, squirrel bites can transmit disease and cause bad infections.

Although people don't usually use the color green to describe the Grand Canyon, it is home to 1,750 plant species. That is more than in any other national park in the United States. Cliff-rose, Apache plume, grizzly-bear prickly pear, mariposa lily, and desert columbine bloom throughout the canyon and give it color.

Grizzly-bear prickly pear

One reason for the variety of plants and trees is the many different climates within the canyon. The canyon is so deep that the climate changes depending on where visitors are.

Each different climate supports different kinds of plants and animals. This is what is known as a biotic community—a group of plants and animals that live together in a certain area. There are six different biotic communities within the canyon.

They too are stacked one on top of another like layers in a gigantic cake.

At the floor of the inner canyon, the climate is desert-like. In the summer the temperature may reach over 105 degrees. The floor gets only eight inches of rain a year, so desert plants like cacti and yucca thrive there.

Agave plants bloom once every fifteen to twenty-five years. They are found deep in the canyon. The plant's flowers, leaves, stalks, and sap can all be eaten. It is sometimes called the "century plant" because it takes so long to bloom. The banana yucca blooms every two or three years and produces a fruit that tastes a bit like bananas.

The creatures that live on the canyon floor, such as kangaroo rats, desert iguanas, and cactus mice, have also adapted to the harsh environment. They can survive in extremely hot, dry weather.

A very different biotic community is found on the canyon's North Rim. It is covered with pine

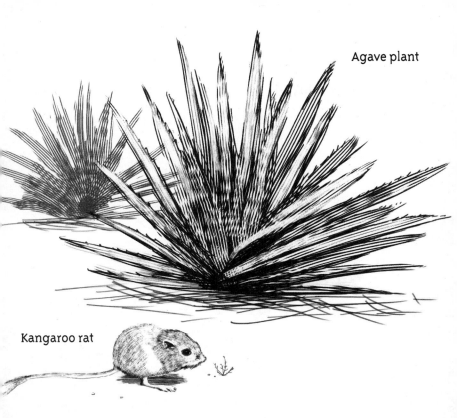

Agave plant

Kangaroo rat

trees and is home to mountain lions, elk, and bighorn sheep. The North Rim gets an average of thirty inches of rain and snow every year. That's a lot. In fact there is so much snow on the North Rim of the Grand Canyon that it is closed to tourists from October to May. All that precipitation, however, is necessary for ponderosa pines, Douglas firs, and spruce. The roots take hold in cracks in the sandstone so that the trees can grow.

Many North Rim animals could not survive in the hot desert conditions of the canyon floor. Likewise, the plants and animals that thrive deep down in the canyon would not survive the rainy, cold North Rim winters. Although the difference in climate is like traveling from Mexico to Canada, amazingly these biotic communities are only a mile apart!

CHAPTER 7
A Trip to the Grand Canyon

Visiting the Grand Canyon is amazing—and frustrating. It's amazing because there are so many sights and so many interesting things to do. (If you've never ridden a mule, you can do that at the Grand Canyon.) But it's frustrating to go there because the Grand Canyon is so huge that seeing only a little bit of it can take two or three days. People visit the Grand Canyon year after year and never see all of it.

Most visitors, especially the first time, go to the South Rim. It is much easier to get to than the isolated North Rim. It also offers a greater choice of things to do and see. Inside the visitor center there is an information desk staffed by park rangers who can answer questions about the park.

The first thing, of course, is to stop and take a good long look. The Grand Canyon Visitor Center on the South Rim by Mather Point is a popular stopping point. The view from there encompasses almost a third of the Grand Canyon.

Before You Go

If you and your family are planning to visit the Grand Canyon, spend some time planning your trip in advance. Visit the National Park Service Grand Canyon website at www.nps.gov/grca. It gives lots of suggestions about how to get to the Grand Canyon, where to stay, and what sights are of special interest. The website also has photos, slide shows, maps, and multimedia presentations.

Mather Point also overlooks one of the widest parts of the canyon. (Remember, if you're visiting during the busy summer months, you may encounter big crowds all along the South Rim. There is plenty of parking away from the rim.)

There are free shuttle buses on the South Rim. The buses take four different routes. Using the shuttle buses is a good way to visit the most-popular spots. It is especially helpful during the busy summer season when one of the roads is closed to regular traffic.

Grand Canyon Village has hosted visitors for over one hundred years. When the Santa Fe Railroad first reached the South Rim in 1901, people finally had an easy way to travel to the Grand Canyon. That's when tourism really began.

At the top of the Bright Angel Trail, visitors cannot miss seeing a rambling frame house with a sign that says *Kolb Studio*. The Kolb brothers, Ellsworth and Emery, also deserve some of the credit for turning the Grand Canyon into a popular vacation spot. In 1902, they started photographing tourists starting their mule trips into the canyon.

Once each group left, one of the brothers, usually Emery, would take the exposed film and scramble nearly five miles down the Bright Angel Trail to where there was freshwater that they needed for processing the film. After developing and printing the pictures in a darkroom they had built there, Emery would walk back up the very steep trail and sell the pictures to the returning tourists.

The Kolbs also roamed throughout the canyon photographing the natural wonders that most tourists could not get to. They sold those pictures in their studio.

In the winter of 1911–1912, Ellsworth and Emery retraced John Wesley Powell's journey down the Colorado through the canyon. They made movies of their trip. In later years they toured the United States, showing the film and encouraging everyone to come and see the Grand Canyon. And many did!

Today the Kolb Studio is a gift shop, bookstore, and art gallery.

In the 1920s and '30s, the architect Mary Jane Colter designed six beautiful buildings for the park. Back then it was unusual for a woman to be an architect. Mary Jane Colter was a very talented one. She took great pains to design buildings

that reflected the Native American history of the Southwest. In fact, she became an expert on Native American customs, art, and jewelry.

Colter designed Hermit's Rest, Desert View Watchtower, and the Lookout Studio to give visitors great places from which to view the Grand Canyon. Lookout Studio is in Grand

Lookout Studio

Canyon Village. Hermit's Rest is seven miles west of the village. Both blend into the canyon landscape so perfectly that it is easy to miss them at first. The rocks in the stone walls are laid horizontally and echo the rim's rock layers. The Desert View Watchtower is twenty-five miles east of the canyon. It looks like an authentic Native American structure, as does Hopi House, the gift shop designed by Colter that is right in the village.

Colter designed two famous hotels at the Grand Canyon—Bright Angel Lodge and Phantom Ranch. Bright Angel Lodge is right in the village. However, Phantom Ranch is at the bottom of the canyon at the base of the Bright Angel Trail. While Phantom Ranch was being built, Colter had to take a five-and-a-half-hour mule ride down to get to the construction site. All the materials for the ranch, except for stones, had to be carried down by mules.

Mary Jane Colter

Besides the six notable buildings in Grand Canyon National Park, Colter designed hotels, restaurants, and shops throughout the southwest United States.

She was born in 1869 in Pittsburgh, Pennsylvania, and studied at the California School of Design in San Francisco. In 1902 she took a summer job with the Fred Harvey Company, which was working with the Santa Fe Railroad building hotels and restaurants. In 1910 she began working for the Harvey Company full-time. Mary Jane Colter designed many other buildings outside the Grand Canyon, but sadly only a few remain. La Posada Hotel in nearby Winslow, Arizona, is the finest of them. She died in 1958.

Mule rides remain a popular way to see the Grand Canyon. Mules have carried supplies and people to the bottom of the canyon and back for over a century. Besides overnight trips to Phantom Ranch, there are shorter mule rides along the rim trail.

Hiking and camping are both popular pastimes in the Grand Canyon. They offer a great way to take in the natural beauty of the area "below the rim."

The most popular hiking route is the Bright Angel Trail. It starts in Grand Canyon Village and twists and turns for 9.9 miles until it reaches Bright Angel Creek and the Colorado River.

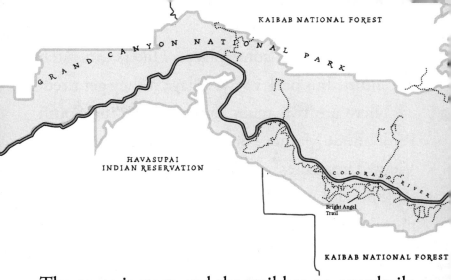

The route is steep and the trail has no guardrails. Hikers must wear good shoes or boots and carry plenty of water because of the extremely high temperatures at the canyon floor.

Even longtime hikers do not try to go down to the river and back in one day. It is also possible to take shorter hikes on the Bright Angel Trail with turnarounds at 1.5-, 3-, and 5-mile points.

Other popular hiking routes are the South Kaibab Trail, Hermit Trail, and Grandview Trail. The easiest trail is the Rim Trail; it goes from Grand Canyon Village to Hermit's Rest. It is flat and even paved in some places. Hikers can catch the shuttle bus back to the village if they get tired.

There are two main campsites on the South Rim, one at Mather Point and the other at Desert View. These sites are operated by the National Park Service and fill up during the busy summer months. Spots at Mather Point can be reserved

through the National Park Service.

Another popular camping site is at Havasu Falls on the Havasupai Indian Reservation. After hiking ten miles down into the canyon, campers pitch their tents next to Havasu Creek.

The North Rim of the Grand Canyon is much more isolated than the South Rim. It has only one hotel, the Grand Canyon Lodge, and one campground. The North Rim is also at a higher altitude than the South Rim and gets much more rain and snow. The North Rim is only open from May 15 to October 15.

Every year thousands of adventurous tourists take raft trips through part or all of the Grand Canyon. The Colorado is a much tamer river now than when John Wesley Powell led his group through the canyon. That's because the Glen Canyon Dam regulates the amount of water in the river.

Seeing the Grand Canyon from a raft is very different from seeing it from the North or South Rims. The canyon walls really seem towering; they look much taller when you gaze up at them from the canyon bottom rather than looking down at them from the rim. And although there are many white-water rapids along the route, experienced guides make rafting trips safe and fun.

CHAPTER 8
The Hand of Man

It is easy to visit the Grand Canyon and think that except for a few buildings here and there, humans have left it alone. But that is not true. The Colorado River has been tamed by dams built at each end of the Grand Canyon. Hoover Dam on the Arizona-Nevada border created a gigantic reservoir called Lake Mead. Lake Mead has flooded the western end of the canyon. It is 112 miles long and over 500 feet deep. The fierce Separation Rapids that so frightened John Wesley Powell and his men were buried by Lake Mead.

At the eastern end of the Grand Canyon is Glen Canyon Dam. It was completed in 1963, and has had a major impact on the canyon's ecology. Many of the canyon's natural sand beaches have disappeared. Spring flooding used

Glen Canyon Dam

to bring new sand down to the beaches. Now that sand is caught behind the dam.

Water is released into the canyon every day. The amount varies depending on how much electricity is needed by the dam's customers. The water has an average temperature of forty-five degrees winter and summer. That's cold!

The humpback chub, a native fish, was able to survive the cold water in winter, but it needed warmer water in the summer for spawning (mating). The fish had to find smaller, warmer side streams to spawn. As a result there are only a few thousand humpback chub, a fish that has lived in the Grand Canyon for three to five million years.

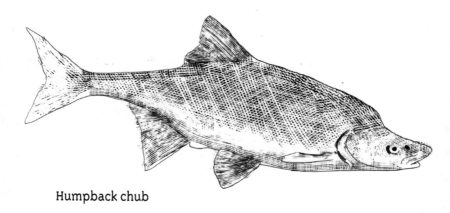

Humpback chub

Now the Park Service is taking steps to protect the humpback chub. It is moving some chub to other streams where the fish will have a better chance at spawning.

Three other species of fish native to the Grand Canyon were not so lucky. The Colorado pikeminnow, roundtail chub, and bonytail have disappeared from the area entirely.

The Grand Canyon's popularity has also created problems. Over a million cars and buses bring tourists to the Grand Canyon each year. In the busy summer months all those vehicles create traffic jams and pollute the air. There are many more people who would like to camp than there are campsites, and keeping the campsites clean and litter-free is not always easy.

In recent years, the Park Service has created a master plan to manage all the visitors. People must park away from the canyon and take shuttle buses to the popular sites on the South Rim. Hikers are no longer able to buy water in disposable plastic bottles anywhere in the park. Camping permits must be obtained in advance, and there is a long waiting list for permits to take private trips down the Colorado. This is to make sure that there are never too many people in the canyon.

President Theodore Roosevelt understood that it is a crime (he called it "vandalism") "to destroy or to permit the destruction of what is beautiful in nature, whether it be a cliff, a forest, or a species of mammal or bird." The rules set down by the Park Service will help keep the Grand Canyon beautiful for everyone now and in the future.

meline of the Grand Canyon

bya= billion years ago, mya=million years ago

- Vishnu Schist forms
- Grand Canyon Supergroup forms
- Bright Angel Shale forms
- Redwall Limestone forms
- Hermit Shale forms
- Kaibab Limestone forms
- Colorado Plateau begins to form
- Colorado River begins eroding the Colorado Plateau to form the Grand Canyon
- First humans visit the Grand Canyon (Paleo-Indians)
- Anasazi begin visiting the Grand Canyon
- First Europeans (Spanish) reach the Grand Canyon
- John Wesley Powell explores the Grand Canyon
- John Hance becomes the first white man to settle at the Grand Canyon
- Theodore Roosevelt is president of the United States; he later becomes known as the "conservation president"
- Santa Fe Railroad reaches the Grand Canyon
- El Tovar Hotel opens
- Mary June Colter begins designing buildings in the area that will become Grand Canyon National Park
- Roosevelt creates Grand Canyon National Monument
- Grand Canyon named national park
- Hoover Dam completed; Lake Mead begins to form
- Glen Canyon Dam completed; Colorado River is "tamed"

Timeline of the World

bya= billion years ago, mya=million years ago

Sponges and jellyfish drift in the sea —

Worms, the first creatures with —
nervous systems, begin to appear

The entire land surface of the earth merges into —
a single continent, known as Pangea

"Continental drift" results in our present —
arrangement of six continents

Mammals appear on earth —

Dinosaurs die out for still-unconfirmed reasons —

Australia becomes a separate land mass —

Various ape species develop the ability to walk upright —

A species of human in east Africa, *Homo erectus*, is —
probably the first identifiable ancestor of modern man

Humans first walk to the Americas across a land bridge —
joining Asia and North America

Hernando Cortés defeats the Aztecs at Tenochtitlan —

Abraham Lincoln takes office as the sixteenth —
president of the United States

World War I begins —

Construction on the Golden Gate Bridge begins —

The state of Israel is officially created —

The first airplane lands at the geographic North Pole —

Fidel Castro leads a revolution in Cuba —

Nelson Mandela is jailed in white-ruled South Africa —

Bibliography

Berke, Arnold. *Mary Colter, Architect of the Southwest.* New York: Princeton Architectural Press, 2002.

Dolnick, Edward. *Down the Great Unknown: John Wesley Powell's 1869 Journey of Discovery and Tragedy Through the Grand Canyon*. New York: HarperCollins, 2001.

Fishbein, Seymour L. *Grand Canyon Country: Its Majesty and Its Lore*. Washington, DC: National Geographic Society, 2011.

Kaiser, James. *Grand Canyon: The Complete Guide: Grand Canyon National Park*. Chicago: Destination Press, 2011.

Newman, Lance, ed. *The Grand Canyon Reader*. Berkeley: University of California Press, 2002.

Website

United States National Park Service, Grand Canyon National Park www.nps.gov/grca/